If Kurt Vonnegut and Erma Bombeck married and had children, their daughter would likely be somebody like Barbara Jones.

Nothing is sacred in this surrealistic satire for the new millennium. Barbara Jones takes a tongue-in-chic look at California political correctness, and flays the nonsensical paradigms of a dysfunctional society with a keen wit and a wryly perceptive flair such as the world has not seen since Joseph Heller.

While she's breaking your funny-bone, she'll shine a new light into the corners of your mind with a refreshing glimpse of what might have been, and what might be!

MOONLIGHT BOWL MANIFESTO

A CURE FOR CALIFORNIA

A Novel by
Barbara Jones

RUSSELL DEAN and COMPANY, Publishers
Santa Margarita, California U.S.A.

Moonlight Bowl Manifesto
A Cure for California
by
Barbara Jones

First Printing : October, 2000

Copyright© 2000 for BEJ Limited (Barbara Jones) by Russell Dean & Company.

Published by Russell Dean & Company, Publishers, 22595 K Street, Santa Margarita, California, 93453-0349. All rights reserved. No portion of this book may be reproduced in any form without the express written consent of the publishers.

This is a work of fiction. All characters and events depicted in this work are fictitious, and any resemblance to real persons, living or dead, is purely coincidental.

Library of Congress Cataloging-in-Publication Data.

Library of Congress Catalog Card Number: CIP **99-069093**

Jones, Barbara (1947-)
Moonlight Bowl Manifesto, A Cure for California/Barbara Jones   p.cm.—
(Russell Dean fiction –novel)

1. Novel. 2. Satire. I. Title. II. The BeachBag Library

ISBN 1-891954-16-4

The BeachBag Library

Russell Dean books are printed on acid-free paper, and meet the guidelines for permanence and durability of the Committee on Production Guidelines for Book Longevity of the Council on Library Resources.

ROCKY RACCOON by John Lennon and Paul McCartney
Copyright© 1968 Sony/ATV Songs LLC. All rights administered by Sony/ATV Music Publishing, 8 Music Square West, Nashville, Tennessee 37203.

All Rights Reserved   Used by Permission

Printed in the United States of America.

RUSSELL DEAN and COMPANY, Publishers
Santa Margarita, California U.S.A.

DEDICATION

Dedicated with love to

Thomas R. Jones

For his infinite patience.

Although he sometimes marches to a different drum,
His heart keeps a true beat.

ACKNOWLEDGMENTS

I've never had faith in my own ability, so others have had faith for me. For this, I would like to thank them. My mother, Celeste Lindstrom, the bravest person I know, believed all her children could fly, if only they flapped hard enough. My father, George Lindstrom, died before he could write his book, but I know he looked over my shoulder and smiled as I wrote this one. My siblings, Mary Ann, Greg, Jeff and Judy have always supported my efforts.

Moonlight Bowl Manifesto would not have seen print without the support of a group of talented writers who critiqued my work and kept me honest: Toby Singhania, who always saw the big picture and nagged me incessantly for new pages; Bobbie Christmas, an editor who cuts with the precision of a surgeon but possesses the spirit of a poet; Jane Mitchell, a true Southern Lady, who can write an entire chapter while waiting at a stoplight; Harriet "Happy" Wall, who provided therapy and a place to create; Phil Flores, a gentleman with an enlightened point of view; Sheila Ward, a determined young woman who will achieve whatever she attempts. Thanks also to Chris Huff, whose room-rocking laugh made me believe I was funny.

I could not write an acknowledgment page without recognizing my friend of twenty years, writer Carla Schanstra, who never fails to ask "So, what have you written lately?"

A special thanks goes to Bradd Hopkins who had the courage to publish a book that forks a little left of main stream.

Barbara Jones
Roswell, Georgia, 1999

⌘⌘⌘

MOONLIGHT BOWL MANIFESTO

A CURE FOR CALIFORNIA

A Novel by
Barbara Jones

RUSSELL DEAN and COMPANY, Publishers
Santa Margarita, California U.S.A.

MOONLIGHT BOWL MANIFESTO

CHAPTER 1
EXPOSURE

Lance Cornell noticed the pig in his swimming pool before he noticed his fence was missing. Lance always admired the pool, his second proudest possession, as he sipped his breakfast energy drink. He admired his proudest possession as he shaved it every morning.

He didn't know whether pigs could swim, so he wasn't sure if the trespasser was pig paddling or pig drowning. He tapped sharply on the picture window of his breakfast nook to get the creature's attention. The interloper responded with rude choking noises and a frightened release of body fluids into the crystalline water. As a yellow cloud swirled through the wake of the thrashing farm animal, Lance bolted through his back door.

As Lance sprinted the few yards between his door and the pool, it occurred to him that his yard was bigger than it had been the day before. It was much bigger and filled with unfamiliar landscaping. He froze mid-sprint and gazed in horror at his surroundings. Sometime during the night, all of the fences on his block had disappeared.

⌘⌘⌘

Ping! What a great sound her vitamin A tablet made as seven-year-old Serene Bright flicked it with thumb and forefinger from its place in line on the kitchen counter. She watched it ricochet from the Waterford vase to the Erte print to the floor, where it was greedily ingested by the patiently waiting Goethe, whose toenails made their own ricocheting sounds on the imitation terrazzo.

"Good Goty!" Serene congratulated. "That was six. Only two more to go." The flatulent old bulldog belched his permission to continue. He was accustomed to this game. They played it every time Serene had her non-custodial-parent weekends with her father.

Each night, Harmony Bright—whom Serene had been instructed never to call Dad, Pop, Father, or anything so possessive—would lay out an array of astrologically approved health intensifiers for Serene's morning consumption. Every morning, while her dad and current guest slept in, Serene played her game of Astro Smash with Goty.

"I don't know why Harmony thinks I need all of these vitamins, Goty," Serene continued as she placed her chin on the counter, level with her recommended daily requirement of vitamin C. "It works better if you scrunch one eye reeeal tight and flick your finger realfast." Serene let fly the sunshine vitamin. Goethe farted, and clattered after it.

The forty-pound marksman eyed the remaining missile, a calcium tablet that she guessed must weigh at least five pounds, too big to swallow, even if she wanted to. She had special plans for this one. She had accidentally discovered that, if stepped on, the tablet crumbled into a fine white powder, just like the "special medicine" in the Lalique crystal bowl on Harmony's bureau. She had even saved her straw from the last trip she and her mother, whom she *was* allowed to call Mom, took to McDonald's. She wanted to do it just right.

MOONLIGHT BOWL MANIFESTO

Goty cocked his wrinkled old head as Serene used an airline-sized bottle of Chenin Blanc as a pestle to work the calcium into a powdery pile on the bottom of a Ming bowl.

"Now Goty, this is not for you to try. This is a very special medicine for relieving stress," Serene echoed her father's words as she edged the powder in neat little snail trails on the marble chopping block. "You mustn't tell your mother, or you might lose visiting privileges." Goty whined as his weekends-only mistress shoved a straw up her button nose. Serene aimed her straw at the snowy lines, looking more like a one-tusked walrus than a second grader, but before she could inhale, a piercing shriek and Goty's frantic barking drew her attention to the back window.

The child chewed a strand of rodent-colored hair while she stared in delighted wonder through the slats in the mini-blinds. Serene had a serious decision to make. She knew she would be in trouble if Harmony didn't consider this important enough to be awakened at seven a.m. on a Saturday. She had to risk it, even if it meant another session with the therapist discussing, "Why you want to ruin your father's love life to get even with him for emotionally abandoning your mother." This was too important. This was monumental!

"Harmony, wake up!" she called as she tried to outrun her own feet and stumbled her way up the stairs to the bedroom her father was currently sharing with someone called Sherie. "Harmony, someone's drowning a pig!"

Harmony was startled awake by a sharp pain in his chest. Two heavy front feet belonging to a bulldog with bad breath were firmly planted on his breastbone. The rear paws kneaded his crotch. His daughter bounced from Reebok to Reebok at the foot of his bed, in flagrant disobedience to the no-entry-to-Harmony's-bedroom-without-permission rule. He punched the audio button on his talking clock and brought his Rolex to eye level for confirmation of the mechanical voice. She was also breaking the pre-nine a.m. non-disturbance rule.

"What pretend game are you playing now? We don't have a swimming pool?" Harmony grumbled through morning phlegm. He squinted bloodshot eyes to bring his fidgeting child into focus. When he could see her clearly, Harmony asked the first question that came to mind. "Why the hell do you have a straw up your nose?"

CHAPTER 2

IRWIN

Irwin Schwep's propensity for hypothecation first exhibited itself prenatally when fetal Irwin postulated that, if his mother would only yell a little louder and push a little harder, he could see a lot sooner what all the bright lights and commotion were about. When he was nine, Irwin theorized that, since chickens had wings, their inability to fly must stem from lack of inspiration, opportunity and instruction. To prove his theory, he spent the entire summer between the fourth and fifth grades flinging angry, confused chickens high into the air from the roof of the coop only to watch them flap frantically and ultimately to the crap-covered ground. Undaunted by failure and the occasional and untimely barbecuing of his laboratory specimens, Irwin insisted that, given more time, those fuckers would fly. His father applauded his perseverance. His mother washed his mouth out with soap.

Thirty years later, Irwin circled the sacrificial barstool slowly, his fingers absently scratching the exposed belly between his relaxed-fit jeans and his shrunken T-shirt. If the first time wasn't a fluke, as everyone assumed it was, it should happen again any minute now. The guys had had a field day with his latest failure, "Now here's an invention we can really use," they had teased, vamping outlandish schemes to take advantage of his botched experiment. "Better luck next time. Score one for the termites—zero for the exterminator."

Irwin didn't mind his buddies' razzing so much anymore, "Watch his eyes," they'd point at him, "there's an idea drifting by. He sees it. See if he can catch it. Damn, he breathed and blew it away." They mocked his intense concentration as he worked to perfect a formula in his greasy garage workshop. "Listen, you can hear the gears grinding away in his head." They meant no harm. They were just being the guys—four strangers who had found each other in a strange land.

Bambi Bennet-Ross-Martin-Schwep hated all of her husband's friends. She didn't like the influence they had over Irwin. They dropped by unannounced, waving six-packs in the air, disrupting Irwin's work. Community property laws might argue that Irwin Schwep owned fifty percent of the compact California-ranch house he shared with his bride of one year, but, because Bambi had received the house in settlement of her first divorce, they both knew who the real landlord was.

So far, she had been able to contain the beer-burping contests and dirty joke telling to the garage workshop, but recently Irwin had been exhibiting signs of an unattractive confidence, and Bambi was afraid he might actually invite some of these softbodies into her home. She had avoided outright refusal by claiming wet carpeting, wet linoleum and wet paint.

The guys knew she was all wet, but didn't blame Irwin. Their generation had grown up with the mystique of the California blonde: free spirit, free love, free sex. Irwin had discovered too late that marrying the myth did not include a free ride, free rent or a free lunch. But she did look good in a leotard —not that the guys had seen her wear anything else—when she allowed herself to be seen at all.

Bambi considered anyone not personally summoned by her an intruder. And because she never invited anyone inside, she never had to worry about wasting money on home improvements. After all, a house is an investment, not an amusement. It's senseless to spend money on furniture that only a few people see when she could spend that same money on a Lexus that thousands could see her driving every day. And if she were lucky enough to get caught in a traffic jam, she and her car could be admired even longer. She certainly wasn't going to dip into her facelift fund so that a few provincials from places called Kansas and Illinois would have a comfortable place to plop their uninvited, untoned behinds.

Irwin looked up from the barstool when he heard Bambi struggling to open the warped door from the kitchen to the garage. He reluctantly left his experiment to push the door open for her. Irwin had once offered to fix the door, but Bambi's bewilderment at the idea of making a repair to a house that wasn't on the market caused Irwin to remark dryly to one of his buddies later, "She keeps reminding me that it's her damned house. If she wants to let it fall down around her, swell."

"Are they gone?" Bambi asked, her tone reflecting a distaste usually reserved for cockroaches and cowpies.

"You can stop pretending you're waxing all the floors in the house. They went to the bowling alley so they would have a chair to sit on and a pot to pee in."

"An alley is a good place for them. Just look at this." Bambi gingerly retrieved a crushed Budweiser can from the trash barrel next to the door.

"Aw come on, Bams, you're not being fair. They hit the bucket almost every shot. Milty scored twelve points."

"I'm surprised Milty didn't eat the cans. Don't they know that aluminum containers pollute the environment? They belong in the recycling bag, not the trash. My god, Irwin, don't they care about the ecosystem?"

"Right now, Bams, they probably only care about emptying their bladders and picking up a spare. You could have been a little friendlier."

"I wasn't expecting visitors. You should never have told them to drop by anytime. They actually believed you meant it."

"I did mean it, Bams," Irwin said peevishly. "Where I was raised, we *like* people to drop by. It's called visiting."

"But I wasn't prepared."

"You get prepared for tax audits and Christmas dinners, not for friends." Irwin sighed as Bambi withdrew into the interior of the house. Almost immediately, Jane Fonda's voice over the VCR was ordering Bambi into positions Irwin only dreamed about in the bedroom. Anxious to shut Jane out and return to his barstool vigil, he gave the doorknob a powerful tug.

"The tug felt 'round the world," he'd call it later in his autobiography *Just A Regular Guy*. The slamming door caused the door jam to shake. The thin garage walls, which rested on, but were not attached to the concrete floor, vibrated in protest. A rusted hubcap, disturbed by the quivering walls, fell from its bent-nail hook and rolled ominously toward the high oak barstool Irwin had earlier saturated with his latest formula. With his hand frozen to the doorknob and his breathing suspended, he watched the dented disc wobble toward and, finally, gently tap a barstool leg.

Sawdust. Irwin's breath returned in a gasp as the disintegrated furniture settled to the floor. All that remained of the erstwhile stool was a pile of oak-colored sawdust and a few wood screws, just like the first time, when the guys had laughed so hard when he leaned against that first barstool and landed in a dusty heap on the garage floor.

"Perfect, Schwep, you're a fucking genius," Leon had helped Irwin to his feet and slapped the dust off his friend's backside with an oily car rag. "Most exterminators would have invented a formula to get rid of the termites. You invent one that gets rid of the wood instead. Were you a breech baby by any chance?"

Irwin had grinned his embarrassment and wiped his dusty eyeglasses. "Something went wrong. I must have transposed numbers. Or maybe some of the chemicals went bad."

"Too bad it was only a fluke. We might have had a real winner here. Liquid Chain Saw, or Stump Thumper! Dissolve your roots and amaze your friends," Irwin's buddy, George, an ex-cop, handed Irwin a broom and dustpan. "Hide the evidence before Bambi charges you for the stool."

Irwin had remained silent as his buddies came up with outrageous scheme after improbable plot. If they had been watching his eyes this time, they would have seen another idea start to drift by, get caught, and begin to grow in Irwin's brain— an idea so vast his temples pulsed!

Irwin knew all along that he could duplicate his experiment. He always kept exact notes of his formulas and procedures, so even his failures could be recreated. He wanted to be sure before he told anyone. As soon as the guys left, he sneaked out another barstool while Bambi silk-screened environmental posters on the patio. When the second chair disintegrated into sawdust and screws, Irwin knew it could be done. He'd work out the details later. Right now, he had to tell the guys. A small, dry, dusty whirlwind was created by his draft as he exploded joyously from his garage and sprinted in the direction of the Moonlight Bowl.

BARBARA JONES

CHAPTER 3

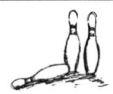

THE PLAN

You could identify the place blindfolded: the lingering odor of a hundred sloshed beers ground into black-and-red-swirled carpeting by the soles of rented shoes, the faintly medicinal, slightly musky aroma of the shoes themselves (sprayed between rentals for your protection); and the greasy-cheesy smell of french fries and nachos clinging to the stained acoustical ceiling and molded plastic furniture. Moonlight Bowl was a little seedier than eastern bowling alleys; not trendy enough to be painted teal and mauve or feature a selection of sparkling waters. This was a gathering place where down-sized electrical engineers, Filipino drug dealers, and night-shift workers avoided sterile apartments and micro-waved enchiladas. Irwin's friends felt safe here. The explosive clatter of falling pins muffled their voices as they continued with the plans they had been making since Irwin's discovery six months earlier.

"If you're gonna have a revolution, you gotta have a slogan." Leon glanced down the alley and noted on the score sheet that Milt had picked up the seven-ten split. "Good going, Milty, my man!"

"What are you talking about, Leon?" George asked, as he snapped a congratulatory towel at Milt's behind.

"A slogan. A motto. A call to arms. 'Remember the Alamo,' that kind of shtick. Hey, I'm up! Earl Anthony, eat your heart out," Leon plucked an ebony sphere from the ball return rack, made a great show of positioning his body and fired the ball down the lane.

"We're not running a goddamned ad campaign here, Leon," George spit on his stubby pencil and recorded Leon's strike.

"This is serious business."

Leon danced back to his seat and checked the scores. "You got spit on the score sheet again. You don't spit any better than you bowl. Revolution is always serious, but I bet all those South American countries have something inspiring to yell when they revolt," Leon asserted.

"Yeah, but 'Death to the Yankee Imperialist Swine' doesn't work for me." George signaled the waitress for another round of beers.

"I'll work on it," Leon pacified. "Anyway, you're up, George."

"I don't want to be up. I don't want to bowl. I hate bowling. Why do we always have to meet in bowling alleys anyway?"

"Because 'they' never bowl. They play tennis, they jog, they arobicize, they surf, but they never, *never* bowl. It's an Eastern sport, something we Easterners do when it's too cold to do anything else."

"Who's an Easterner?" George asked. "You're from Detroit. I'm from Chicago."

"It's what the natives call anyone who lives east of Las Vegas. Anyway, their mothers warn them away from bowling alleys when they are still yupperinies. Besides, this is where Schweppy first told us his plan. He feels comfortable here. No Bambi sending psychic hate messages to us through the walls."

"I like to bowl."

"I know you do, Milty, old buddy, and you do a hell of a job," Leon tried unsuccessfully to encircle Milt's massive shoulders with his right arm. He settled for an affectionate punch instead. "We're not saying that bowling is bad, it just ain't *chic*."

"Are you calling me a hick? I've taken enough crap from these people without *you* starting in on me." Milton twirled his bowling towel into a stinging whip.

"Relax. Here, have a beer," George placated with a Budweiser snatched from the tray of a passing waitress wearing the nametag, 'Sunshine,' over her breast pocket.

"Hey, I mean, like, that's not your beer, you know," the skinny barmaid protested nasally.

"Yeah, well, like, you're not our waitress, so that makes us even. By the way, where the hell is our waitress?"

"She went home. She had, like, a headache. You know what I'm saying?"

"Okay, so where's our beer?"

"Like, how would I know? I mean, you're not like my station, you know what I'm saying?"

"Ooookayyyy," George drew out his syllables and mentally counted to ten. "Since you have to go back to the bar and replace the brew I just gave to my man, Milty, why don't you pick up another round and drop it off here?"

"You'll like have to wait for Rainbow. She's, you know, your waitress. If I get your beer, Rainbow will go all 'Why did you take my station?'"

"I thought Rainbow had a headache."

"No, that was Moon. Rainbow is like, you know, her replacement. She'll like be here after her, you know, audition."

"She has to audition for a waitress job?" George asked.

"Like, don't be stuuupid. She's like, you know, an actress. So am I, you know."

"Shakespearean?"

"Supermarket. I mean, I like, want to be the person, you know, who hands out the little hot dogs on toothpicks, you know, and those great itzy bitty, like, paper cups with wine samples, and like, who knows, you know, someday I could be in, like, a taste test."

"I like a woman with a dream," Leon interjected, "but right now, I'd prefer a woman with a tray full of brewskies."

"Sorry, you're like, not my station, you know. You like owe me a buck fifty for the drink you stole."

"Here you go, Lady MacBeth," George tossed two singles on her tray. "Keep the change for like, you know, diction lessons."

Smiling her thanks for the tip, but wondering who this Lady MacBeth person was, Sunshine aimed her skinny body toward the other end, her end, of the building.

"Who says we don't need a revolution," Leon nodded his head in the direction of the departing Diction Queen. "Another obvious case of brain burn."

"Don't be too quick to judge," George cautioned. "Schweppy has a theory about people like our celestial friend."

"Irwin has lots of theories," Milt offered between gulps of beer."

"That's why we love him," George countered. "Anyway, he says that scientists claim that humans—and you too, Milty—use only ten to twenty percent of their brains. He believes that the remaining eighty to ninety percent of our brains send out energy to help run the universe. The less you use your brain to function here on earth, the more you are involved in maintaining the planets and the solar systems. In other words, the dumber you are, the more important you are to the cosmos."

"So what you're saying," Leon surmised, "is that Sunshine is not really stupid…"

"…she's just busy running the universe."

CHAPTER 4

MILT

Milton Lefkowitz thought being a guerrilla would be a whole lot tougher. "Hell, this is a snap," Milton whispered into the garage-sale tape recorder attached high on his muscular left arm with black electrical tape, giving the impression that he was talking into his armpit. He hadn't intended to tape it so close to his shoulder, but when his uniform arrived, its short sleeves proved inadequate for concealing a recorder taped to his wrist. He'd really hoped for a cell phone, or at least a walkie-talkie, but funds were tight. Considering the magnitude of the plan the guys had been working on for a year, and what it had done to their cash reserves, he'd settled for the fuzzy recorder.

"I've been in more danger hanging out in the old neighborhood," Milton informed his armpit. As soon as "this thing with the natives" was over, he was planning to find someone to write his autobiography for him. It wasn't that Milton wasn't bright enough to pen his own glorious epic; he figured he'd be just too busy with his new job.

The promise of a real job had convinced Milton to join the revolution in the first place. He wasn't even clear on what "this thing with the natives" was all about, but because he had been assured that no one would be harmed, he figured "What the hell, I can't be any worse off."

One thing Milton did know for sure, he was damned mad at himself for buying into the whole California myth. At first, he had tried to blame Vinnie, but ultimately he knew he must take full responsibility for believing this "laid back, good life" bullshit.

⌘⌘⌘

"Vinnie, I hope you choke on your fucking guacamole," had been Milton's parting shot to his ersatz buddy from the old neighborhood. The trip from New York to California had devoured Milton and Marge's life savings, what with the cost of the rental trailer, food for themselves and the kids, repairs to the fourth-hand Buick purchased specially for the trip, and souvenirs for the poor suckers they left behind on Delancey Street.

They hadn't worried, though. Vinnie had painted a golden picture of the good life. Milton and Marge were both strong. In high school they had been voted "Couple Most Likely to Work on the Docks." If they both worked their butts off they could make a good wage working on his avocado ranch, Vinnie had assured them, and then quickly turn those wages into a fortune by investing in real estate. However, while the Lefkowitzes were blindly heeding Horace Greeley's counsel to "go west," the inadequacy of the U.S./Mexico Border Patrol was affording Vinnie "Reneger" Ratkowski a fresh opportunity to live up to his nickname.

In the interim between Vinnie's invitation and the Lefkowitzes' arrival in California, possibly while Marge was mopping up vomit from three carsick kids somewhere outside South Bend, Indiana, Vinnie had discovered quasi-legal slave labor —illegal aliens. The Lefkowitzes were suddenly priced out of the market.

"Milty...Margie..., what a joke on...," Vinnie's final words were indistinguishable, coming as they were from a mouth filled with the largest, ripest avocado within Marge's reach. "Hey, Jerkface," Marge flung over her shoulder to the poor suffocating bastard she had once called her friend. "Just be glad you weren't growing watermelons!"

Often, in the next few months, Marge regretted not keeping the avocado she had so impulsively rammed down Vinnie's gullet. More than Vinnie deserved to choke, she, Milton and the kids deserved to eat. Pride, and the code of the old neighborhood, precluded their sending home for money, particularly when "So long, suckers, see you in the movies,", had been their farewell speech to the troops gathered at Polaski's bar for their farewell blast. No one back home suspected that she, Milton and the three kids were currently living in what the newspapers facetiously called "the only low cost housing in the Bay area," a 1967 Buick.

It wasn't that they weren't trying. There would be no welfare for the Lefkowitz family. They both had jobs, but they worked for minimum wages. Milton was a night watchman at a hazardous waste dump and Marge worked days building burritos at a taco stand. But, Sister Ignacio's axiom notwithstanding, hard work does not always reap its own rewards. They couldn't afford a place to live without wheels.

Any landlord who condescended to rent to people carnal enough to produce multiple offspring compensated by requiring the first and last month's rent, plus a large security deposit before allowing occupancy. Minimum wage, even times two, when used for food, gasoline and payments to Casa de Mini Storage for stowing their furniture, didn't allow much saving for security deposits. Milton actually broached the subject of living in Casa de Mini-Storage with the night manager. Hell, he figured, he was already paying for the space, his furniture was already there, and it beat the hell out of living in the 1967 Buick. The manager was neither sympathetic nor receptive. He had a minimum wage job to protect, too.

Milton clicked off his tape recorder. A familiar urgent sensation had turned his attention from his memoirs to the guerrilla's curse. He had to piss. He reconnoitered his surroundings, the suburban backyard of a split-level Santa Lolita, California, home.

It had been ridiculously easy to gain entry to most of the yards. Milton had run into more obstacles trying to get in to see human resource managers than he had sneaking into twenty backyards in broad daylight. He had been assigned an "upwardly mobile" neighborhood, which meant that all the adults in the family held full-time jobs to support their upwardly mobile homes.

The kids should have been a problem, but it seemed that the ones who weren't sitting glued to the television screen, downloading porno from the Internet, or still in daycare, were convinced by his work clothes and gardening tools that he wasn't someone worth paying any attention to. They were too busy hurling rocks at the Neighborhood Watch signs to notice that he never actually used any of the tools he carried except the leaf blower, which, instead of blowing leaves, sprayed liquid. Even if they had noticed, they would merely have assumed he was a lazy illegal. Their preoccupied minds registered his gardener's clothing but not his wide, white Polish face.

High wooden fences and lush shrubbery successfully shielded his activities once he closed a gate behind him. He had been worried about dogs, and carried a pocketful of tranquilizer-laced ground beef, but he'd only run into one dog in twenty yards and that pooch had declined the beef and followed him around like a long-lost friend. "Damned yuppie puppies, probably only eat whole wheat dog biscuits and piss Perrier," he

MOONLIGHT BOWL MANIFESTO

muttered to himself.

"Jesus, Mary and Joseph, what the hell is that?" Milton stabbed frantically at the "on" button of his recorder, forgetting for the moment his need to urinate. "Jesus Christ and all His Apostles, it's a real gardener!"

This was great! This was really great! Finally, Milton had something dangerous to handle and record for posterity. "Hey you," Milton addressed the legitimate gardener as the man wrestled a wheelbarrow through a narrow gateway, "you don't work today. Go home!"

"Today Friday. I work here Friday. I work today." The elderly Asian refused to be pushed around and doggedly dragged his wheelbarrow toward the shrubbery.

"No, they forgot to tell you. It's a holiday. No one can work today. It's a sin."

"Then why are you working, asshole," the old gentleman thought but didn't say as he surveyed Milton's coveralls. *"You'll soon be sweating like a pig, wearing polyester to work outside."*

Mistaking his deliberate silence for acquiescence and, wanting to be helpful, Milton propelled the barrow toward the gateway. Remarkably, he suddenly found himself on his back in the juniper bushes. "He must have used some kind of ju-jitsu," a chagrined Milton confided to his armpit as he struggled to regain his feet and his dignity. "I wasn't trying to steal your shitbox old wheelbarrow, you washed out old kamikaze pilot; I was helping you leave. No workee today, amscray! What does it take to make you understand?"

"I work today, make twenty-five dollar," the dignified old man intoned quietly in the pidgin English he knew Americans expected of him.

"If I give you twenty-five bucks, you'll go?"

"You give, I go. No checks."

Milton fished two wilted tens and a fiver from his pocket and presented them with a bow to his worthy opponent. His honorable foe returned the bow, grabbed the handles of his barrow and made a stately exit.

"What a schmuck," the real gardener muttered in perfectly clear English as he continued down the driveway to his truck, "always smelling his armpits. That's what he gets for wearing polyester in this heat."

Painfully reminded of his need to relieve himself, Milton once again surveyed his surroundings. "Too late to observe the niceties," he said, hopping from one foot to the other. With apologies to his sainted mother, Milton headed toward the swimming pool, unzipping his fly as he walked.

CHAPTER 5

MARGE

"Hold still! If the manager comes in here before we're finished, he'll throw us right out, and the whole world will see your shiny hiny," Marge admonished lovingly, adding a pat to her daughter's tiny behind for emphasis. Three-year-old Lois Lefkowitz was standing nature naked in a sink at a K-Mart store and loving every minute of it. This was the closest her family had come to the beach since arriving in California.

"No! Mama, hurry! I'll be still." Lois had the procedure down pat. She stood, with the soapy support of her mother, in a wash basin, with one diminutive foot firmly planted over the drain hole to keep the water from being sucked away before she was done with it, while her four-year-old sister Lenore held the faucet handle in the "on" position to keep it from shutting off automatically, a feature the store had installed to curtail vandalism. A few minutes earlier, their positions had been reversed. Five-year-old Leonard Lefkowitz stood guard outside the bathroom door to signal the approach of anyone wearing a store identification badge.

"Isn't it awful?" Marge confided to a well-dressed woman looking disdainfully at the child who was now making rude faces at herself in the spitwad-covered mirror. "Ten miles from home, and she decides to spill a giant Slurpy all over herself," Marge lied as she dabbed at her slippery daughter with a handful of paper towels.

"Ouch, Mama! Use the fluffy one," Lois protested, referring to the bath towel her mother had just used to dry her sister and then hastily tossed into an open stall when she heard someone enter the ladies room.

"Shssh, Baby," Marge silenced. "You know we only use

that towel when we have our bath at home," she tried to recover, ears reddening with humiliation. The woman she was trying to impress, however, had tired of their cozy vignette and studiously picked her teeth in the mirror.

"But, Mother," Lenore piped up plaintively, dismayed that her sibling had been unjustly chastised, "we don't have a ho..." Before Lenore could broadcast the dreadful truth, a frantic pounding, Leonard's signal, spurred all three into action.

Lenore crawled under the door and unlocked the empty stall they had reserved for just such an emergency, not noticing in her panic that there were three stalls open and vacant. Lois jumped from the sink to her mother's back as Marge bent over to grab the plastic shopping bag containing soap, toothpaste and brushes, clean clothes, and other paraphernalia which would immediately brand them "homeless." They'd been through this drill before and were safely hidden in their re-locked stall before the outside door closed behind the entering store employee. A tiny wet hand reaching under the partition from one stall to another to retrieve a fluffy purple bath towel would be all that the cashier could have seen if she'd been paying the slightest bit of attention to anything but herself.

Awkwardly, in their cramped hiding place, Marge dressed Lois, sometimes unintentionally bending fragile knees and elbows in directions they weren't meant to bend. Clothed, they would appear to be typical shoppers and could pass unnoticed through the crowd. However, while tying frayed laces on worn-out sneakers, a terrible scene played in Marge's head. She imagined she and her children were standing at the checkout counter when the voice of Vinnie "Reneger" Ratkowski boomed over the P.A. system, "Attention K-Mart shoppers, the Marge and Milton Lefkowitz family is living in a 1967 Buick."

CHAPTER 6

VIVICA

"Take your time. It's just another tacky production number," Vivica yelled as she jabbed the mute button on the remote control. She was answered by a loud flushing noise, followed by the slight sucking sound of magnets being pulled apart. "Don't forget to put down the toilet seat. And stay out of my medicine cabinet. You don't fool me by running water, I can still hear the door open."

"Since when did Joan Collins die and leave you Queen Bitch?" Lance whined as he entered Vivica's bedroom from the master bath. "I only wanted a Valium. You have a gallon full, for Christ's sake, Viv. Are we having a little visit from the PMS fairy?"

"You would know better than I. He's a relative of yours, isn't he?"

"Yes, Sweetie. Just like the Tooth Fairy and all the Sugar Plum Fairies. But, we all know who the real Nut Cracker is here, don't we?"

Vivica fluffed and then patted the pile of pillows next to her on the king-sized bed. "If you weren't my very best friend, I'd take offense at that remark."

"Oh," Lance grabbed a pillow and punctuated his reply with soft blows to Vivica's head, "and I'm not supposed to take offense at those fairy remarks? Oh God, oh God, oh God, turn it up, turn it up!" Lance dropped and rolled over Vivica's body, snatched the remote control and turned up the volume before landing on the floor next to Viv's side of the bed. From the thirty-five-inch screen, a voice bereft of male hormones was emanating from a body scientifically mutated to androgyny.

"It *is* him. It's Ricky Johnson." Lance waved the remote

at the TV. "God, his false eyelashes are so huge it looks like tiny bats are sucking on his eyeballs."

"Jealous?"

"Oh, please. He's got so much plastic in him, when he dies he won't be buried, he'll be recycled."

"He must be pushing forty." Vivica squeezed hand lotion into her palm and passed the bottle to Lance.

"Pushing? He's dragging it behind him...on a long rope." Lance slathered silky lotion up to his elbows.

"Phanny doesn't like him."

"You promised you'd leave Phanny inside tonight. It's bad enough when you let Margaret Mitchell out. All that suing talk."

Epiphany Enchilada (Phanny to her friends) was Vivica Lakeland's newest personality. Viv had been living with Margaret Mitchell in her psyche for years; so while the arrival by astral plane of a new identity was annoying, it wasn't a shock. Phanny, however, was not thrilled to find herself sharing a body with Margaret Mitchell and a lawyer. She was a flower child, an old organic, the kids would call her, the antithesis of everything Vivica stood for.

"I don't let Margaret out," Vivica said. "She comes out whenever she damn well pleases, and I'm starting to lose control of Phanny, too. They're talking to each other. Now Phanny's talking about a lawsuit.

Unlike Phanny, Margaret Mitchell had been delighted to find her incarnated soul in the body of a lawyer; or so Vivica's hypnotherapist had told her. Margaret Mitchell needed a lawyer. Now that she time-shared a body with one, she could finally take care of Alexandra Ripley. She'd already taken care of "the dump"—that depressing old apartment building where she'd written about Rhett and Scarlett. Margaret had cajoled Vivica into visiting the Atlanta tourist attraction while on a business trip. A little lighter fluid, a carelessly tossed cigarette and *pooff!*, the dump was gone with the wind. She had been forced to admit that, although an immortal soul is a wondrous thing, a body with fingers to strike matches and feet to flee a crime scene was pretty handy, too.

"Who's Phanny suing? The person who named her, I hope."

"Me, Lance. Can you believe it? She wants to stop publication of my book."

"*How to Evict Your Parents and Remain in Their Will?*"

"No, the new one I'm writing with my hypnotherapist about my multiple personality disorder, *I'm Okay, I'm Okay, I'm Okay.* She doesn't want to be in it."

"How does Margaret Mitchell feel about the book?"

"She thinks it's great as long as I tell the world that she's mad as hell about the sequel to her book."

"Such language from a southern lady."

"Phanny's teaching her."

"Well, fiddledy-freaking-dee."

Lance flipped his stringy body from the floor and nestled into the down comforter next to Vivica to watch the television event of the year.

Vivica Lakeland and Lancelot Cornell had been best friends from the time they had played Barbies together as children. Viv had always preferred Lance over the dirty, rough little boys in her neighborhood. The two had become blood brothers when they were both eleven and pricked their fingers in a secret, solemn ceremony in the crawlspace of the house Lance would later inherit. Although Vivica had moved away after her first marriage, she often came back between husbands to confide in Lance, and visit his grandmother in the rest home. In exchange, Lance occasionally checked in on Viv's mother, who still lived at the end of the cul-de-sac. This way neither of them had to deal directly with family members, and Viv didn't have to pretend to love her father. Tonight, they were at Vivica's big new house in Los Greedos, pretending they were orphans.

"There's something wrong with your clicker, Viv." Lance pressed the volume bar on the remote control device and stretched his arm toward the TV. "Who the hell's that?" He wiggled to the foot of the bed and peered at the man who had replaced Ricky on the screen. "Clacky, clacky, clacky, Viv. What in the world is he wearing? What happened to Ricky? Where's the music?" Lance thumped the remote with the heel of his hand. The television set was quiet except for some strangling, throat-clearing noises.

"Stop smacking my controller. There's nothing wrong with the set. He's probably a representative from the charity, or maybe he's a charity case. He's wearing a bowling shirt. Bowling shirts are retro-chic, not clacky."

"Nothing's retro-chic anymore, Vivkins. Anti-chic, maybe. But, I still say he's Classically Tacky. So out, he's in."

"Hi, I'm George," the man finally announced at full volume from Vivica's set.

"For Christ's sake, Lance, turn down the sound."

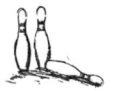

CHAPTER 7

THE ANNOUNCEMENT

Security was as tight as Milton's cummerbund. Irwin had promised he'd only have to wear the monkey suit until George made the announcement. That would still be longer than Milton had worn a tux at his own wedding to Marge. Management had supplied the tuxedos, a fact for which Leon, the Easterner's bean-counter, was thankful. Management had also screened all personnel working the auditorium that evening and had not noticed, nor would they have been surprised or alarmed by the fact if they had, that not one employee was a native-born Californian.

Milton opened the limo door and grabbed the arm of the hefty comedian. Looking at her pasty white skin, platinum hair and three-hundred-and-fifty-pound body stuffed into a silver lame gown, Milton couldn't help thinking of a baked potato in aluminum foil, topped with a dollop of sour cream. He was hungry. Revolution was hard work, and he'd been popping people out of limos like corks out of wine bottles for nearly two hours. The new auditorium held three thousand people, and every celebrity had been given an arrival time. The bigger the star, the closer to curtain time they arrived. As Milton reached into the long white car to retrieve the potato's wrap, he noticed several empty vials half buried in the thick lamb's wool floor mats. He, Marge and the kids could live comfortably for months on what those drugs must have cost. Hell, he reflected, he, Marge and the kids could live comfortably for months in that limo.

A sudden surge of the ogling crowd, and the screech of

wooden barricades scratching pavement as they were pushed closer to the gods, brought Milton back to homeless reality. Chelsea Dove had arrived. And so had Milton.

⌘⌘⌘

George Lindstrom hadn't considered stage fright. He'd imagined a swat team, or an angry audience surging on stage to disembowel him. He hadn't dreamed that his own body would betray him. He had been picked to make the announcement because he was Mr. Cool—the one who could always make the guys laugh. Leon was too black, too threatening, they figured. And Milton was, well, he was Milton. People liked George. He was not too blond, too tall, or too good-looking.

George thought Irwin should have had the honor. After all, it was his discovery that had made this day possible. But Leon and Milty were afraid Irwin would start spouting one of his theories and the audience would fall asleep.

George's voice was lodged somewhere between his diaphragm and his mouth, like a giant burp. He tried punching himself between his nipples to dislodge the speech he had worked on so hard, then jammed his hands deep into his pockets to wipe off the sweat on the lining. He couldn't understand these physical manifestations of fear. He wasn't afraid. This was only a game, something Irwin and he had come up with to entertain the guys. Any second now, Irwin would run on stage, pull him off, and they would all have a good laugh reading about the nut who had crashed the Really Big Night of Stars Telethon. When he turned stage left, seeking deliverance from the wings, the words "Moonlight Bowl" blazoned across the back of his pumpkin-orange shirt, stitched in an arch over a smiling quarter moon inscribed in an embroidered bowling ball.

MOONLIGHT BOWL MANIFESTO

"Uh-oh. Choke city." Milton, watching from the wings, held his cummerbund and bow tie in one hand and was undoing the buttons of his starched white shirt with the other.

"He'll be fine in a few seconds." Irwin waved at George and gave him the thumbs-up sign. "It's just a momentary involuntary muscle constriction. His subconscious is afraid, even if George doesn't have the sense to be."

"Well, I think his subconscious is about to wet its pants." Milton tossed his cummerbund and tie, removed his shirt and bent over to untie his shoes.

"What the hell are you doing?" Irwin asked.

"I remember someone saying something once, like, if your audience was naked, you wouldn't be nervous." Milt was stripped down to white briefs and black dress socks. A Velcro band attached his tape recorder just above his wrist. He had given up fastening it with electrical tape after the first time he yanked the tape, and a thousand hairs, off his arm.

"Once again you're close, but no cigar. The speaker is supposed to *imagine* the audience naked."

"Oh." Milton was now nude. The cue-card girl fainted and George snapped out of his trance.

"Hi. I'm George." George pulled his still slightly-damp hands from his pockets and waved at the audience. To keep the announcement friendly, but firm, he had decided to start with a joke. "You're all grounded!" In a charitable mood, the audience laughed politely, although they began to shift in their chairs and glance at their gilt-edged programs. "You won't find me listed as part of tonight's entertainment, except maybe under ...*And Many More Surprises*."

The baked potato—Marguerite to her adoring fans, her agent and her three ex-husbands—simmered with rage. She had been standing backstage, watching a monitor and waiting for Monty Griffin, the emcee, to give her her cue, when George ambled on stage instead. "Grounded, shit. I'll grind him...into sausage," she vowed as she pounded toward center stage. The sight of Milton bending over to pull up a pair of faded jeans, momentarily diverted her attention, and her hormones. She thought she had seen that face someplace before, but she knew she had never seen that spectacular butt. She made a mental note to investigate after she got rid of the hick in polyester who was literally stealing her limelight.

Until he felt the chubby hand on his shoulder and sharp fingernails skewering the flesh on the back of his neck, George Lindstrom had assumed the thunderous applause was for his wit. "Smile, maggot man," Marguerite whispered into George's ear as she hugged him like an old friend. "And tell me why I shouldn't sever your jugular."

George extricated himself from her grasp. "Ladies and gentlemen, it's Marguerite!"

"Great! It's just like the Asian gardener," Milton informed Irwin, and then his wrist recorder. "An unexpected challenge! Only she speaks English." Milt thumped the flickering light on the small recording device and hoped the batteries would hold out.

Marguerite laced her fingers under her chin, smiled, and batted her eyelashes at the audience. She had originally assumed this pose whenever photographers were around, using her hands to hide some of her chins. She did it so often, it had become her trademark.

"Isn't she wonderful?" Couldn't you just hug her to death?" George drew her close. Loud clapping and gratuitous laughter covered their voices. "I'm sorry, but either you get off

MOONLIGHT BOWL MANIFESTO

this stage or the big man over there in the wings will push a button and blow up this entire auditorium. Now, wave bye-bye to the nice people."

Marguerite looked stage left and saw Milton Lefkowitz fiddling with the controls on his tape recorder and watched Monty Griffin, trussed and gagged, hop from behind a stack of props and tumble squirming in his ropes at Lefkowitz's feet. The hunk with the sumptuous butt a terrorist? She looked back at George. He nodded and smiled. Marguerite obediently waved bye-bye and walked zombie-like off-stage where Milton, for the second time that day, firmly took her arm. "Wasn't she wonderful, ladies and gentlemen? Thank you, Marguerite. We'll all be looking for your new movie." George led a round of applause.

His ex-cop brain told him to stop a second and reassess. What was really happening? Irwin wasn't coming to his rescue. A fat lady had tried to kill him. Okay, he had handled it. For some reason, Milton had stripped naked. That hadn't been part of the plan, but he was dressed now, and had Marguerite restrained. *"'Once more unto the breach, dear friends, once more.' When in doubt, quote,"* he thought.

"I want to thank all of you for coming here tonight to support this worthy cause. I also want to thank the gazillion of you who are watching us on television. I specially want to thank those of you who are calling in to make pledges to help those afflicted by this dread disease." With a sweep of his arms, George indicated the banks of telephones stage right, each phone manned by a confused minor celebrity who hadn't the foggiest idea who the hell George was.

Chelsea Dove was bored. Her publicist and her probation officer had insisted she accept the invitation to appear at this event to try to mend her tattered public image and fulfill some court-assigned community service obligations. Could it get any more tedious? First, some Neanderthal had yanked her out of her car so hard her shoulder pad had flipped into her armpit; then they confiscated her cellular phone at the door because it might interfere with the life support systems of the telethon poster child. Now, a left-wing liberal nut case was about to go on interminably about some no-nuke, whale-saving, anti-fur-coat, pro-Native-American bullshit. It was bad enough she would be forced to watch a parade of cripples, and maybe even be forced to hug one. She prayed this wasn't a disease that drooled.

"I encourage you to keep these phones ringing," George continued. "However, I am going to interrupt the scheduled program for a few minutes to make a little announcement." He smiled nervously and coughed behind his hand to clear his throat.

Chelsea groaned. "Here comes the Sacheen Little Feather bit. Where the hell is security?"

"I am not a Native Californian." George stepped back two paces and hung his head.

"I knew it," Chelsea thought. "It's the Native-American schtick."

"But I love California!" He stepped forward to cheers from the audience. "However," George paused for effect and for the cheering to subside, "California is in trouble."

"It's definitely the no-nuke thing." Chelsea raised the middle finger of her hand behind her program, stood up and started knocking knees and stepping on feet as she pushed toward the aisle.

At a signal from George, a curtain behind him parted to reveal a large movie screen. A banner, hand lettered by Leon

MOONLIGHT BOWL MANIFESTO

with the words *Nolite Exspoliare Facultatem*, swung precariously above the screen. Below the banner, the parted curtain revealed a scene of bucolic bliss: a copse of trees with leaves waltzing gently to the strains of Handel's *Water Music* as robins hopped sociably from branch to branch twittering bird gossip.

"Excuse me, Miss Dove." The usher at the rear door of the auditorium blocked Chelsea's exit. "We'd like very much for you to stay for the rest of the speech."

"And I'd like very much for you to get the hell out of my way."

When the usher didn't move, Chelsea was tempted to make a scene, but then remembered her probation and returned to her seat.

"California is blessed," George said, "with scenery and weather and talent and spirit. Yet half of you are starving yourselves and the other half are having the flesh peeled back from their faces and sutured into new positions." George pulled the skin at the corners of his mouth in grotesque imitation of a face lift. "You name your children after soap opera characters and you don't know the names of your next-door neighbors. You put your grandparents in nursing homes, then hire nannies to watch your children." George shrugged. "Something's wrong here. You're not real people, you're figments of the rest of the world's imagination, images on a screen, electric shadows."

Confused audience members squirmed in their seats, consulted their programs and waited for the scheduled entertainment to start.

"But, like Pinocchio, you can become real." George gestured theatrically toward the woodsy scene behind him. Handel's *Water Music* was drowned out as loud cymbals crashed, and traumatized birds abandoned their perches. The copse of trees shimmered for an instant, then disintegrated into a pile of timber dust and coughing squirrels. A hand appeared across the screen as the cameraman wiped fine wood particles from his lens.

The audience laughed. Marguerite relaxed and allowed herself to enjoy the pressure of Milton's strong hand on her arm. This was obviously a publicity stunt to promote a new movie. She put her free hand on Milton's forearm and pressed her hip against his thigh.

"This is not a movie," George shouted impatiently over the laughter, embarrassed by the response to his dramatic moment. "That was not a special effect. It's a remote hookup." With a few more snorts and chuckles, the audience settled down.

"You are all now hostages," George said. *Shit, that's not how I wanted to say it,* he thought when he heard frightened gasps from the audience. "Guests!" he said aloud. "You'll be our honored guests for a little while."

Marguerite casually took her hand from Milton's arm and surreptitiously released the catch on her diamond necklace. She hunched her shoulders, and the gems slid easily into the Grand Canyon between her breasts.

"My friends and I," George went on, "came West to share a dream and found a coma. We're here to bring you to your senses, not hurt you. Please be aware that two out of five of you here tonight are Easterners, in on our plan." At George's signal, hands went up throughout the auditorium as Eastern infiltrators identified themselves. "Throughout the state, the ratio is the same. We are not violent, but we are serious."

George turned once again to the screen behind him, where the scene had changed to show a huge tree. "This is

MOONLIGHT BOWL MANIFESTO

General Sherman, the world's most massive living thing. It lives in Sequoia National Forest and is two hundred and seventy-two feet tall with a trunk thirty-five feet in diameter and one hundred-nine feet in circumference at the base. It contains enough timber to build one hundred twenty houses. As you saw in the earlier scene, we have developed weapons that can pulverize on command." George raised his arm as if to signal destruction of the treasured tourist attraction.

"No!" The audience screamed in unison, except for Chelsea Dove, who wondered if this hostage time would count toward her community service hours.

"Okay." George lowered his arm slowly, thankful no one had called his bluff. The smaller trees had been saturated with Irwin's wood disintegrating liquid and videotaped several days earlier. Irwin's discovery, dubbed Offence, took at least twenty-four hours to work and the exact time of meltdown could not be pinpointed. The giant sequoia had not been sprayed. "As long as you cooperate, General Sherman is safe. Remember, though out of sight, these weapons are everywhere, and you'll never know who can pull the trigger or what will disappear next."

"Before I leave you to think about what I've just said, let's check the tally. These phones have been going nuts." George turned toward the long tables where glitzy volunteers scribbled furiously, conferred with each other and pecked at computer keys. The giant tote board hadn't changed since George had begun his speech.

"Excuse me....uh, George?" Last year's Mr. Universe held up a handful of pink slips. "It's about all these pledges..." Taking courage from his leadership, the others waved dozens of similar forms. "They're all for you."

35

"What?" George walked over to the table.

"Yes, George, Sir. A man in Enid, Oklahoma, says he'll send you Easters five-hundred dollars if you make Monty Griffin admit publicly that he wears a toupee," he read on, "and one thousand if you make him take it off." In the wings, Monty grunted through his gag and tried to slither back behind the props.

George grabbed the paper from Mr. Universe to read for himself. "We're Easterners, not Easters," he corrected. But it was too late. With one slip of the tongue the revolutionaries had gotten a name.

Mr. Universe continued. "A woman from Bucksnort, Tennessee, pledges to match the amount of money she's spent on diet pills, diet plans, diet tapes and non-fat, non-taste food, if you'll make it a law that any leading lady must weigh at least one-hundred-ninety-five pounds."

Backstage, Leon, the keeper of the Easters' meager accounts, was doing backflips.

"The Governor of Oregon promises all the money allocated by his state for pollution control if you promise to keep Californians from crossing the border and inflating property values in Oregon. And a woman from our own state will write a check tonight for ten-thousand dollars if Alexandra Ripley will tell the worldwide viewing audience that she is sorry for writing *Scarlett*." Last year's Mr. Universe looked puzzled by the last request, but recovered quickly. "All the calls are like that." He grinned. "They're all with you!"

Milton and Irwin hugged each other. Marguerite hugged Milton.

"Mr. George. There's a phone call for you." Another volunteer held up a phone receiver.

"It's just George. Not Mister. I'm a little busy. Take a message."

"They say it's the White House."

"And now, a word from a few of our many sponsors." George signaled the director to break and took the phone.

"Hello. This is George."

"Well, you must know who this is."

"Yes, Sir. I recognize your voice, Mr. President."

"Well, you certainly have got yourself a tiger by the tail, George."

"Yes, Sir."

"I suppose you want to negotiate."

"No, Sir. I...I mean *we*, only want to help."

"Well, here's the deal. It's all yours."

"Sir?"

"California. It's all yours. Me and the boys in Congress have been trying for years to figure out what to do with those loonies on the left coast. Other than sawing the state off at the border and floating it out to sea, we haven't come up with anything. Don't expect any interference from us. Good luck. Stay in touch."

Click. Dial tone.

BARBARA JONES

MOONLIGHT BOWL MANIFESTO

CHAPTER 8

LOVE IS BLONDE

Bambi picked her causes carefully—a lot more carefully than she picked her husbands. Four years of art school, plus three summers studying at the Sorbonne had equipped her well for life as an environmentalist/shop keeper. Eighty thousand tuition dollars had prepared her to silkscreen the most eye-catching, heart-wrenching picket signs in the state. The time she had spent in Paris helped her hone the shopping skills she needed to fill the display shelves of Victorianarama, her financially failing but high-profile shop, with useless, albeit expensive, antiques and collectables. She considered antiques recycled human artifacts and was proud of the fact that she wrapped every delicate collectable sold in recycled newspaper and put it in a bag made of recycled paper bearing the shop's logo. She had designed the logo herself, Queen Victoria's profile over a banner proclaiming "God Save The Rain Forest."

Bambi was unconcerned that she never turned a profit. None of the stores in the redwood-shaded, tourist-swollen little village by the bay made any money. Most of them were tax write-offs for the wealthy husbands of bored women who thought it might be fun to own a little business of their own. Bambi's first husband had funded Victorianarama. Shop hours in the village were erratic, opening and closing times subject to buying trips, tennis lessons, face-lift healing time, spring skiing season, affairs with delivery boys or, in Bambi's case, protest demonstrations. She had even painted a sign for her front window "Closed to Save the Earth." Displayed below the sign was an enlarged newspaper clipping showing her being led away in handcuffs. The caption read, "Local businesswoman defends the rights of endangered larvae."

Bambi's first marriage had been for money. At her mother's urging she had married young, while her skin still fit tightly and her breasts still pointed north. Her first divorce had left her with her ranch home, her shop and enough income to support the losses her shop posted every month. Her second marriage had been for lust, but her second spouse had snug skin and impressive pecs, too, and soon left Bambi for a woman with more money, a bigger house and a firmer form. Her second divorce left her with an obsession for workout tapes and fat-free food.

Bambi met Irwin while she was picketing the pharmaceutical company where he worked. Unlike the management of his company, Irwin had been delighted to see the protesters. He assumed they were protesting for the same reason he was planning to leave the company—they had discovered that management was cooperating with the government in chemical warfare experiments. He was so buoyed by the courageous pickets, he quit his job on the spot and walked out of his laboratory to join the marchers.

"Murderers!" Bambi's sign had screamed, the death-black letters dripping appropriately in blood-red acrylics.

Irwin fell in beside the most beautiful blonde he had seen in a state full of beautiful blondes and offered to carry her sign. "I really admire what you are doing," he told her. "I was hoping someone with brains would finally figure out what was going on inside. No one would listen to me. They call me a 'disgruntled employee.' You could be saving millions of lives," Irwin told her as he lifted her sign high for the television cameras.

MOONLIGHT BOWL MANIFESTO

A strange sensation came over Bambi. She felt something she had never felt before; *smart*. No one had ever accused her of having a brain before, and she liked the feeling it gave her. She took a second look at the man with the Supercuts haircut walking next to her. Not usually her type. Not even someone she'd notice. But maybe, she thought, he had potential.

Two months later, after a dizzying courtship and an impetuous elopement to Las Vegas, as Irwin was cleaning out the garage to make room for a workshop, he noticed the "Murderers" sign in a pile of discarded protest paraphernalia. Thinking it would be romantic to have the placard framed as a symbol of their meeting, Irwin approached his bride.

"What chemical warfare protest, Winnie?" At this point in their marriage, Irwin was still too infatuated to tell his wife that the sobriquet "Winnie" made him retch.

"Bams! The one where we met and fell in love."

"Oh, you mean the mouse killers."

"No. I mean Belushi Pharmaceuticals, which was collaborating with the U.S. Government to develop a tablet that, when dropped in a water supply would cause whole populations to vomit themselves into oblivion."

"Oh, well, war is hell." Bambi thought she was being smart again, remembering a quote she heard in a movie. "I'm talking about Belushi Pharmaceuticals maiming and murdering innocent little white mice in diabolical experiments."

Irwin's mouth fell open as he stared at his wife in startled comprehension. "Sweetheart, laboratory mice are used everywhere for medical experiments. They're grown for that purpose. I used them."

"Irwin!" Winnie had been replaced. "How could you? People make their own problems, mice have no choice."

The honeymoon was over. The problem was, Irwin wasn't bending to Bambi's will. He had the irritating habit of making up his own mind. He had seemed delighted with the health club membership his bride had given him as a wedding present, but when Dax, the behemoth who had shown them around on their first visit, poked Irwin in the stomach and commented, "Well, I can see what we need to work on here," Irwin's face broiled with anger and embarrassment. He never returned.

He always ate the healthy dinner that he and Bams prepared together. However, Irwin considered this meal merely the *hors d'oeuvre*. The main course came later, in front of the TV, and typically consisted of a family-sized bag of potato or corn chips, which Irwin classified as vegetables, and a two-liter bottle of soda. Sometimes he added a pound brick of cheese, which he munched like a candy bar.

Irwin also insisted on dressing himself. He told his wife he'd been picking out his own clothes since he was twelve and would continue to do so. Unfortunately, he was still picking out the same styles he had worn at age twelve, including his favorite horizontally striped T-shirts, which made his potbelly look like a beachball. The guys and the lab rats had never complained.

Bambi tried tennis. But when the club manager told Irwin he couldn't wear his favorite, frayed, black Converse high-tops on the court, Irwin pontificated on elitism and hung up his racket forever.

She tried running. "Think of it as fleeing from fat," Bambi said.

"Fat caught up with me and beat the hell out of me years ago," Irwin replied.

⌘⌘⌘

MOONLIGHT BOWL MANIFESTO

Bambi thought about Irwin as she picketed the Self Center. She had tried to get him to come with her, but he seemed nervous when she mentioned the Center. "Bams, I wish you would stay in tonight." But, she knew the Center would be swarming with press covering the telethon, and she didn't want to miss a photo op to support her latest cause.

"Why? You're going out."

"I told you. I have an important meeting. You'll learn all about it later." Irwin felt guilty keeping Bambi in the dark, but he knew her mouth. She couldn't keep it closed. He loved her, but she *was* a native.

Her protest wasn't getting much sympathy or media coverage. It might have been a bad decision to confront people who were dying and tell them that white mice were being sacrificed so a cure could be found for their disease. She was thinking about going home and watching the telethon on TV when she saw it—a fur coat! Visions of screaming, furry creatures being skinned alive for their pelts swam in front of her eyes. She couldn't resist. She unstopped the bottle of red dye she kept ready in her purse and flung it at the mink-swathed ingenue.

Bambi later thought of pressing charges of police brutality. At the very least, the policeman who arrested her must have hit her hard on the head. As the officer pushed her into the squad car, she hallucinated Irwin's friend Milton, dressed in a tuxedo, pulling a giant baked potato out of a limo

BARBARA JONES

CHAPTER 9

THE GUYS

Marge wasn't getting out of the bathtub, revolution or no revolution. If Nero could fiddle, Marge could bathe. Her sturdy body filled the tub. She had already lathered and rinsed her short dark hair three times, emptying the tiny bottle of fragrant shampoo supplied by the Center. Through the open door, she watched Leonard and Lois enjoying cartoons in the dressing room. Lenore had toddled off to breakfast earlier with her father. Marge savored her time in the tub, knowing that, sooner or later, she and Milty were going straight to hell. It had to be some kind of mortal sin to kidnap a state…Thou Shalt Not Take Three Thousand People Hostage. Saying a few dozen Hail Marys wasn't going to get her off the hook for this one.

⌘⌘⌘

Milton rolled imaginary bowling balls across the stage and nailed imaginary strikes every time. "Damn, I'm good!" he exclaimed to no one in particular.

"Look again," George said. "You left the seven-ten split on that last one."

Milton turned to look, and then grinned at his own foolishness. "Aren't you supposed to be baby-sitting?" George asked. "Where's the Munchkin? Mothers get very upset if you lose their kids."

"I didn't lose her." Unable to keep still, Milton was now shooting invisible baskets. "Lenore wanted to go back to our room after breakfast. I think all these people are making her a

45

little shy. Anyway, I think it's better if she's not here when Irwin gets back with Bambi. Bambi doesn't like kids."

"Unless they're endangered," George added as he leaned back in his chair, creased a sheet of paper into an airplane and launched it stage right.

"Hey!" Leon looked up from the new pile of pledges he was keying into a PC. "You almost put my eye out with that thing."

"It was either that or call in a pledge to get your attention. Haven't you been to bed?"

George and Milton had found Leon already on stage supervising a new group of phone-bank volunteers when they arrived for their morning strategy meeting. This shift, however, eschewed the glittery garb of the previous crew and opted for the comfortable uniform of the Easters. Leon, to distinguish himself as a member of the founding four, wore his Moonlight Bowl shirt, untucked, over a pair of no-name jeans. His big toes wiggled joyously in worn-out K-Mart sneakers each time he entered a new pledge into the system. He was too stoked to sleep. Promises of money had continued all night. Apparently, to a disgruntled world, California represented that smirking teenager everybody wanted to smack in the face, but always had been afraid to. Now, for a couple of bucks, a person could get in a few good whacks.

Irwin appeared, Bambiless, from the wings.

CHAPTER 10
THE MORNING AFTER

The Easters had no intentions of being cruel. They wanted their groundees (hostage was much too harsh a word) to be as comfortable as possible. Even while they were in the first stages of planning the revolution, sweet-souled Marge insisted the captives should have all the amenities she herself had been denied for the past year. So, when Milton left the toxic waste dump for a new job as night security guard on the construction site of Hollywood's latest monument to itself, The Self Center, and brought back glowing reports of a Xanadu without the finesse of a Kubla Khan, the guys knew they had found their location.

The Center sprawled over several hundred acres of land that had conveniently become vacant during one of God's little wake-up messages to California, an out-of-control forest fire. Two years were spent building and outfitting a facility dedicated to self-flattery, self-indulgence and self-promotion. In addition to an auditorium that seated three thousand people, it contained fifty private dressing rooms, each with fully appointed bath including bidet.

"People are going to get one hell of a shock when they flush these toilets," Milton had commented to another guard when he saw the French refinement. A TV with VCR and a refrigerator completed the amenities, although some stars were planning to customize as befitted their status. Two gleaming, chrome and steel kitchens could provide catering for any or all of four banquet halls. A domed stadium for sporting events, a clinic, corridors full of offices, storerooms, power-conference rooms, wardrobe rooms and any other rooms needed to pamper or promote Hollywood's only export made up the rest of the complex. Only when people across the country picketed movie theaters to protest the exorbitant amount of money being spent did the developers of the project pragmatically offer the site as an earthquake emergency evacuation center. Thousands of folding cots, water, flashlights and other emergency supplies were stashed throughout the buildings at the complex. When the protest turned into a boycott, management promised to dedicate one night each year to a celebrity telethon for that year's trendiest cause. When they agreed that the first telethon would be the premier event of the center, the boycott was quashed.

"Were you in a school play?" Lenore Lefkowitz knew the shiny lady was only pretending to be asleep. She had her eyelids squeezed too tight. "I was in a play at my pre-school." Marguerite turned over and buried her head under a pillow. Unperturbed, Lenore skipped around to the other side of the khaki-green cot. "I played a carrot."

"Beat it."

"You look like a princess."

Marguerite peeked through the slits she had allowed in her eyelids. "Not too ugly for a knee nibbler."

"The biggest princess in the whole kingdom."

"Take a sneak."

"I had hot oatmeal for breakfast," Lenore chattered. "They have real stoves here. I have a bathroom no one has to guard. Leonard says this isn't a real house, but it is. Nothing's for sale. We don't have to pretend to shop. Here's your shoes. No one stole them. See? It's safe here." Lenore held out a pair of size eleven evening shoes.

Marguerite perked up considerably at the mention of

food. Today was purple day. She swung her legs over the side of the cot and grabbed at her shoes. Lenore pulled them back against her chest. "What do we say when we want something?" Lenore wheedled.

"Give me my goddamned shoes, or I'll rip off both your legs and beat you over the head with the bloody stumps."

Lenore dropped the shoes. "Ohhh, that's a sin! You're going straight to hell," she said as she shook a tiny, damning finger at Marguerite.

"Yeah, yeah, I'm scared. Where's the dining room?"

The dining room was an uncomfortable marriage of Self Center decadence and Easter practicality. Expensive reproduction Louis XIV chairs had been pushed against the walls. Monogrammed china, silver and crystal had been moved into storage rooms to be saved for "company" by the grandmotherly Easters in charge of meals. Plastic utensils, and paper plates and napkins were good enough for "family." Three gray-haired ladies in hairnets reigned over the cafeteria-style counter that had replaced the stored banquet tables. Diners balancing trays on their knees occupied most of the gilded chairs. A large sign, hanging from a crystal chandelier, directed "You're mother doesn't work here. Return trays to kitchen and throw away your trash." This same scene, with very little variation, was repeated in three other banquet halls.

"Where's the chef?" Marguerite stared at the women. She hadn't seen gray hair outside of a movie set since she moved to California from her grandparents' farm in Iowa fifteen years earlier. She had become so used to seeing touched-up hair, she assumed science had discovered a cure for gray. And the wrinkles. Hadn't these people heard of Retin-A? As a recent investor in Tuck and Suck, a chain of plastic surgery and liposuction clinics, Marguerite was looking forward to her own appointment to have fat vacuumed from her behind and injected into the crevices on her forehead.

"Mildred, Dotty and I did all of the cooking ourselves, Dear. Is there a problem?" The first hairnet spoke.

Marguerite looked up and down the length of the counter and then at the nametag on the old lady's withered bosom. Her publicist had taught her that people responded more positively to you if you used their names. " There's no purple food, Alice."

"Dear?"

"I like purple. Dinosaurs are purple," Lenore, feeling it incumbent upon herself to act as guide to the big princess, added to the conversation.

"Dinosaurs are not purple—unless of course their corpses are rotting in the sun," Marguerite informed the child, whose name she hadn't found necessary to learn.

"Here, Dear, have some purple grapes." The three grandmothers had been briefed that some of these Hollywood types were eccentric, and it was better just to humor them.

"Grapes *are* purple."

"Yes, Dear. Grapes are purple." Alice wondered if she were witnessing one of those LSD flashbacks that she had heard about.

"Don't you get it? Don't you watch TV? It's been on all the talk shows. I'm on the Dye-it Diet. Every day is a different color: Monday, green; Tuesday, blue, and so on. Today is purple; purple pancakes, purple oatmeal, purple scrambled eggs, whatever."

"But why, Dear?"

"Scientific studies have shown that people expect their

food to be a certain color, Alice," the Princess explained patiently in another public relations gambit. "If you were served, for instance, purple mashed potatoes, they wouldn't appear very appetizing. You would eat less."

"But wouldn't you still be hungry?"

"No, Alice. That's the great part. You're allowed to eat as much as you want. You just don't want to eat as much."

"I think lavender vanilla pudding might be very nice."

"Not lavender. Not mint green. Not nice, pastel lemonade shades. Dark, strangulated tongue or bruise-colored purple, or festering wound green or shit brown. How much pus-yellow milk could you drink?"

"We get the idea."

"Swell, then I'd like a purple croissant, purple pancakes and purple orange juice."

"Goodness, we couldn't do that."

"And why the hell not?"

"If we gave one star special treatment, we'd have to give every star special treatment. And that just wouldn't work, would it?"

"Jesus Christ! I'm ten-years old again."

Lenore crossed herself and said a quick Hail Mary for Marguerite's soul.

BARBARA JONES

MOONLIGHT BOWL MANIFESTO

CHAPTER 11
WHEN PIGS FLY

"The last time Father escaped, we found him stealing bean sprouts from a bin at the organic food co-op down the street. There's no telling where we might find him this time. With a little luck, and a lot of Valium, Mother might not even know he's missing yet." Vivica deftly shifted the cellular phone to her right ear and rolled up the window of the vintage Porsche with her free left hand, closing out the exhaust fumes belched by the bus in front of her.

"What makes you so sure he's missing? Maybe he decided to hang around the house. He must have formed some kind of attachment to your mother by now."

"Don't be silly, Doctor. His beady little eyes are constantly searching out a hole in the fence or an open gate. If Mother's fence is missing, he's gone." Vivica spied an opening in the fast lane and zipped around and ahead of the County Transit bus.

Traffic was light this morning, the usual beach-seeking gridlock delayed or canceled by the catastrophic announcements of the previous evening. The County Transit bus diminishing rapidly in Vivica's rear view mirror was empty except for the driver, one Juan Escobar, who didn't understand a word of English and was blissfully ignorant of the revolution. The rest of the traffic consisted of emergency vehicles, others who hadn't heard the news and a convoy of sparkling white trucks.

"Doctor, I see their trucks."

"How do you know they're Easter trucks?"

"They have the same motto, the one in Latin, painted on

each side."

"Can you get any closer? See if they are carrying weapons."

"I've got to hang up, Doctor. I see my exit." Vivica downshifted across three lanes, noting as she negotiated the off ramp that the conquerors in the white vans were gaily waving goodbye.

Her mother's house was quiet when Vivica shocked her pampered Porsche by slamming its brakes and ramming its front end into the garage door. A cursory examination of the grounds confirmed her fears. The perimeter of her mother's property was now protected with only a line of brownish-gray sawdust, all that remained of her comforting wooden barricade. Father was nowhere in sight.

Awakened by— but not comprehending— the sound of the Porsche impacting the garage door, Veronica Lakeland struggled to pull her drug-worn body into the conscious world. Someone had screwed her eyeballs too tightly into their sockets again; Morpheus, fucking around in his Valium veil, Veronica suspected. One eye now opened, the left still sealed with a combination of pollen, fog and Estee Lauder Swiss Performing Extract, Veronica fought to bring blood to her deadened limbs. A prickly, painful carbonated rush of sensation through her awakening arms and legs let her know that, for today at least, she was still alive. Had there really been a time when her body would awaken as a whole and she would leap from bed refreshed? Veronica doubted those days ever really existed.

Veronica Lakeland lived halfway between reality and the Oprah Winfrey Show. She survived comfortably on the proceeds of the lawsuit filed by her attorney daughter against the sky-diving instructor who had negligently failed to ask the late

MOONLIGHT BOWL MANIFESTO

Mr. Lakeland if he had recently ingested any drugs which might make him believe that "rip cords are for wienies." The house was paid for, and there was money enough for the necessities of life: facelifts; prescription drugs; and a lifetime membership at Rancho Sobrieto, where she could dry out and collect autographs at the same time. Veronica had never approved of her husband's pharmacological hobbies and only used drugs herself to assuage her fears that the insurance company would find out that the late Hamilton Lakeland was not only not late, but he was living in her back yard.

Veronica had wallowed in widowhood. She wore black, emitted brave little sighs, and hinted at self-immolation to join her beloved "on the flames of love." Her grieving eventually took her to a "healing through petting" retreat in the redwoods where the bereaved were encouraged to bond with farm and forest creatures. As she stood staring into the moist nostrils of a cow, Veronica felt a familiar poke at her behind. She had been goosed in exactly the same spot Hamilton had always chosen. "Ham!" she twirled, expecting for a confused moment to see her late husband's grinning face. She saw, instead, a fly-covered, booger-eyed pig staring at her.

BARBARA JONES

CHAPTER 12
HOWDY, NEIGHBOR

Vivica hadn't been in her mother's home since Father had bitten her on the ass. It seemed the born-again Mr. Lakeland made all of his acquaintances from behind. When Vivica pointed this out to her mother in a faint-hearted attempt to dissuade her of the belief that a five-hundred pound Hampshire hog was her late spouse, Veronica pointed out that the original Hamilton had also goosed every woman he met. When the reincarnated Ham Lakeland introduced himself in his usual manner to Lance, Lance had commented that perhaps he was rooting for truffles. The pig had developed this anti-social behavior shortly before Veronica purchased him from Healing Through Petting, Inc. Before she rescued him, he had been scheduled to be the closing *luau's* entree.

As Vivica waited for her mother to get dressed, she stood before a painting in the living room and remembered the first time she had seen it hanging there. "Mother, this can't be a real Picasso." It had looked vaguely Picassoesque, but Viv couldn't recognize the period.

"Of course it is. Look at the signature."

"The signature looks authentic, but I don't recognize the period. It's not his Blue or his Rose."

"It's his Dead period."

"Excuse me?"

"He channels through Baba Raba. He painted it last week. Baba says many of the great painters are getting restless in the ether and are using her earthly body to continue their art."

This made perfect sense to Vivica. "Does she do Monet?"

Phanny thought it was all a pile of crap. Margaret Mitchell

empathized. She knew what it was to have your art violated.

Veronica sat quietly, if not still, while her daughter described the previous nights events to her. Her hands moved continuously, brushing harsh blond hairs away from her eyes, picking at a week-old manicure, twisting rings around her fingers, digging leftover sleep from the corners of her eyes. She had been surprised to see Vivica. Usually, her minion, Lance, made these duty calls.

"Baba Raba prophesied all this." Veronica responded after Vivica finished.

"Baba Raba predicted people in bowling shirts would disintegrate our fences and capture our movie stars?"

"Yes. In her Harmonic Convergence Day predictions, she foretold 'A strike force will break down our barriers and steal our souls.' Same thing. I'll have to tell your father."

⌘⌘⌘

Lance quickly realized that it was Hamilton Lakeland flopping around in his swimming pool. He couldn't imagine what had possessed the pig to take this early morning dip until he saw the oranges, dropped from overhanging branches, bobbing in the water. He'd have to try to save the greedy swine or Vivica would never forgive him. However, if mouth-to-mouth resuscitation were called for, her papa was porkchops. Not that she believed the pig was really her dad, but as long as her mother believed it, Vivica was safe from a new step-father sucking her inheritance dry.

Lance grabbed the skimmer pole and gently patted the pig's hams, hoping to turn him toward the shallow end.

⌘⌘⌘

Serene sat on the high kitchen stool and kicked the counter hard with each frustrated swing of her leg. Her thinking stool,

MOONLIGHT BOWL MANIFESTO

Harmony called it. She was told to sit there until she figured out why she would make up such a wild tale to annoy Harmony and Sherie with on a Sunday morning.

"But it is too true, Goty. I can see them." It wasn't necessary to confirm the fact with the dog. He was frantically trying to scratch a hole in the sliding glass door that led to the back yard. When Goethe saw the monster scramble up the pool steps and head in the direction of his mistress, he launched his enraged body against the door, shattering the glass.

Highly polished pebbles flew as Goty skidded through Harmony's Zen garden, disturbing cosmic tranquility and a thousand dollars' worth of Zen-scaping. He snorted as the familiar odor filled his sensitive nostrils. He had known all along a beast dwelled in the neighborhood. He had smelled it every other weekend when he reconnoitered the back yard to make sure it was safe for his beloved Serene. But the humans had fastened dead trees together to form a wall that prevented him from tracking down the fiend's lair and ripping its throat out. Now was his chance. The wall was gone.

Lance tried hard to stop Mr. Hamilton, but five-hundred pounds of panicked pork bearing down on you is enough to daunt even the bravest Lancelot.

Goty braked to a stop so fast his butt bounced on the ground. He was upon the beast—worse, the beast was upon him. Although pigs are credited with the superior intellect, dogs aren't stupid. Goty turned tail and ran back through the shattered door Serene slid open. Ham followed.

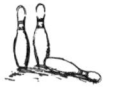

CHAPTER 13

ARMANI, AU REVOIR

Marguerite couldn't lose the kid.

"You forgot to say grace," Lenore accused.

"What do I have to be thankful for? None of this food is purple." Marguerite tapped her fork against the glass of orange orange juice and poked at the yellow scrambled eggs in disgust.

"You have grape jelly."

"You just don't get it, do you kid?" Marguerite downed the glass of juice, cleaned her plate of hash-browns and eggs and ate four pieces of toast with grape jelly. "Where have they stashed my cell phone? I need to have some clean clothes sent over." Marguerite dabbed at a large jelly stain on her silver gown and sniffed her underarms. "My pits have gone bad."

Chelsea Dove hadn't slept. She couldn't sleep in a room full of strangers—with one stranger, yes…she'd done that many times—but not a roomful. She had tried to leave when George began his speech, but they'd stopped her at the door, and she wasn't small enough yet to slip through the cracks. She had huddled all night in a plush auditorium seat, knees to her chest, arms wrapped around her legs, hiding from lights that would expand her body with fattening shadows. If they would leave her alone, she could quietly disappear.

"There you are, Chels." Marguerite loomed over the bone-thin brat-packer. "Come on. This kid's going to show us where we can wash up and get some clean clothes. They won't let us send for our own stuff. Must be something in the Geneva Conventions about that, don't you think?"

"Fuck off, Fatso." If they weren't going to let her disappear, Chelsea was going to have to defend herself. That's all it was—the hotel trashings, the paparazzi bashings—self defense. And Marguerite scared her. She took up so much space. She breathed too much air.

"Watch your mouth, there's a kid here. And her father's your biggest fan. He's some kind of big shot with the Easters. If he likes you, he may not have you disintegrated."

Lenore tugged at Marguerite's gown. She wanted to grab her hand, but was afraid of the long, pointed fingernails, chromed to match her dress. "That's my daddy up there." She pointed to the stage at the front of the auditorium where Milton and the guys were holding their meeting. "He thinks I'm in my room."

"Christ, let's get out of here before her old man sees us and has us shot for kidnapping." Marguerite swept a delighted Lenore into her arms, pulled Chelsea by the elbow out of her fetal position and exited through the massive, hand-carved ebony doors to the lobby. Marguerite was still convinced that the tape recorder Velcroed to Milton's wrist was a detonating device.

⌘⌘⌘

After her leisurely bath, Marge had reported, with two of her children, for her assignment as wardrobe coordinator. Lenore's brother Leonard was busy untangling a pile of wire coat hangers on the floor. Baby Lois busied herself tangling them up again each time Leonard turned his back. For months, the Easters had been combing Goodwill and other second-hand stores and soliciting families across the country for donations of just the right kind of clothing. It had been easy, really. Most people contacted had exactly what Marge's committee was

MOONLIGHT BOWL MANIFESTO

looking for tucked away in the back of closets or stashed in boxes in basements, garages, or attics. And most people were eager to get rid of it. For weeks, volunteers had been sorting donations by size, color and team name, from Ajax Plumbing All Stars to Zachary's Pizza Pirates. Thousands and thousands of bowling shirts now hung limply on racks lining the walls of the gymnasium. Marge, herself, was wearing the distaff uniform of Moonlight Bowl, a neon-pink Moonbeamer shirt. Used blue jeans, minus any labels or stitched designer logos were stacked neatly on the bleachers. The underwear was new. No one, it seemed, packed away old jockey shorts or brassieres.

"This kid says we can get some clean clothes here." Marguerite said.

Marge was startled to see her daughter in the arms of television's biggest sitcom star. She gaped in momentary confusion, trying to separate everyone's favorite wacky TV mom from the glittering, grape-stained ediface standing in front of her.

"Hi, Mommy."

"Shit, I've done it again," Marguerite quickly handed Lenore to her stunned mother. "I didn't do anything to the kid. I found her wandering around, and I've been trying all morning to locate her grieving parents."

"You get one shirt, one pair of jeans and one set of underwear," Marge was finally able to say. "No shoes or socks, so watch where you step. We'll have your gowns and jewelry sent to your homes or back to the designer who loaned them to you. You can pick up a new set of clothes every other day. We'll assign laundry duty later."

"You don't really expect us to wear this crap, do you?" Marguerite pinched a hanging garment and quickly wiped her fingers on her dress. "Oh, my God, it's polyester! I *know* the Geneva Conventions have a law against this!"

"Mama, can I help Aunt Marguerite? I know just the outfit for her." Lenore laced her dainty fingers under her chin and batted her eyelashes in imitation of her newly adopted relative.

"Hey, don't be wading in my gene pool, kid. You ain't no relative of mine without a DNA test to back you up." Marguerite had had her fill of long-lost relatives showing up to share her good fortune and her Malibu beach house. "Well, I guess I could use your help. I'm sure you've got plenty of stuff to fit Miss Annie Rexia here," Marguerite indicated Chelsea standing sullenly next to a mountain of denim. "But, clothes to fit a real woman like me are hard to find."

"Oh, no," said Marge. "For some reason, we got in an exceptionally large number of queen-sized ladies' shirts from the Midwestern states, particularly from Iowa."

"Mama, please, I know just the one." Lenore had helped with the sorting and knew exactly the sort of shirt a princess should wear.

Twenty minutes later, Marguerite emerged from the shower room resplendent as a Lenny's Liquors Light'ning Bug, complete with rhinestone-trimmed pockets and battery-powered, flashing bug behind. Although the Easters had confiscated her gown, shoes, and the diamond necklace that clinked to the floor when she showered, Marguerite had been able to convince them that the device she was still wearing concealed under her shirt was of medical necessity. Girdling her midsection was a soft leather belt, studded like a dog collar with firm rubber spikes turned inward toward the body. The belt was quite comfortable, unless one overindulged, then it tightened and tortured. It could not be loosened. It could only be cut off.

Chelsea wore her usual black, although her usual black didn't usually include the words Strang's Perpetual Care embroidered across the back.

⌘⌘⌘

The Easter dorm monitor hadn't been sure where to assign Ricky Johnson a cot. When it became time for the groundees to turn in, the superstar was still dressed in the costume he had worn earlier on stage, a diaphanous white tunic, slung over one shoulder and falling in loose designer-engineered folds over his hips. Under the tunic, skin-sucking, zebra-striped Spandex pants ended midway between his knees and his Achilles tendon. Dozens of gold ankle bracelets filled in the space between the pant legs and his Chinese silk slippers. His completely hairless body, bat-wing eyelashes coated in mascara and shoulder-length hair styled in a flip put the dorm mother in a quandary. Was this a man or a really flat-chested woman? However, a state of California driver's license and the assurance from a male witness that Ricky did, indeed, pee standing up, led the monitor to the decision to allow Ricky into the men's dormitory.

When Marge saw Ricky in her clothing line the next morning, she wasn't sure if he was a man, woman, or six-foot-tall cartoon. Without his hairdresser and valet, Ricky could not quite pull himself together. During his nocturnal gyrations, his overly teased and processed hair had shifted stiffly to one side of his head. One eyelash had migrated from his eyelid to just above his right nipple, giving the impression his bosom was winking at you. His face was still completely beardless. After he picked out an androgynous shirt and jeans, he headed toward the men's shower room. Marge noticed that the other men in line waited until Ricky came out before they went in.

When he reappeared, he was wearing his tunic wrapped turban-style around his head. Marge knew it was against the rules to allow hostages to keep any of their original clothing, but thought his headdress might have religious significance. Maybe he was some kind of Hindu. She knew he would be having enough problems. All of his bare toes were polished bright red.

CHAPTER 14

THE SPY

Milton noticed the freak before the others. Groundees had been wandering in and out of the auditorium all morning. Irwin said it was okay. He wanted their guests to feel comfortable. Most of them soon got bored watching the invisible bowling and basketball games and wandered off again. They couldn't hear what was being said on stage without microphones. The Self Center had been built for ostentation, not acoustics.

Ricky Johnson was angling for protection. He suspected his superstar status was useless here. Immediately following last night's announcement, he discovered that all his bodyguards were Easters who were now assigned to keeping agents and screenwriters from sneaking into the Center to sign up the guys for movie and book deals. Ricky planned to protect himself the same way he had as a child, by becoming a snitch. He approached the stage cautiously. "Hey, guys, how about an autograph?"

Milton was suspicious. "We don't give autographs."

"I was going to give you my autograph."

"Autograph this, Gunga Din." Milton wound up and threw an imaginary baseball. Ricky ducked. He was offended. The look he had been going for was Norma Desmond, not Rudyard Kipling.

"Give him a break. My daughter loves him." Leon waved Ricky to the stage. "Maybe she'll think I'm cool again if I get a signed picture for her."

Leon had moved to California from Detroit to give his family a better life. What he got was a divorce from a wife suddenly interested in intensifying her aura, and a daughter who would no longer buy clothes on sale because "If they're on sale, it's because the really cool kids didn't want them when they first came out." When he confronted his only child with the joints he found secreted among her designer socks, and she had responded "Jesus, Leon, you're so Midwestern," he had decided to join the revolution. On his last visit to her at his ex-wife's home, he noticed that his daughter's room was papered with Ricky Johnson posters. Maybe he had found a way to score some points.

Leon had heard that California was color-blind—a belief that was reinforced when he found a job as an accountant for a sporting goods manufacturer soon after arriving. He didn't know at the time that California employers jumped at the chance to hire people who still believed that Fridays were part of the workweek, and not travel days for trips to the mountains, beaches or Las Vegas. He had not yet learned that a bad-hair day was an acceptable excuse for calling in sick. He felt encouraged by the fact that he could walk around an expensive department store without a nervous clerk dusting clean shelves as she trailed surreptitiously behind him. He was unaware that Silicon Valley technology allowed hidden monitoring devices to record every move and sound he made the second he entered the mall.

Leon began to question Mother California's all-loving, all-forgiving reputation when a native had warned him, "Watch out for the Beaners. They sneak across the border and steal our jobs." Somehow the *B* word was acceptable where the *N* word wasn't. However, according to other informed sources, Asians had it made on the West Coast. A fellow-worker had crossed his heart and held up his right hand when he swore to Leon that every boat-person who managed to drag himself onto the shores of our thirty-first state, spitting seaweed and blowing salt-water bubbles out of his nose, was given a Seven-Eleven and ten thousand dollars cash.

Ricky Johnson defied any racial or sexual stereotyping. His genetic spiral had twisted itself into a genetic Slinky. His gender confusion deepened when his manager started pumping him full of hormones while he was still a teenager to keep his voice from changing. His nose had been altered so many times, you could hang a hat from the upturned end. The marketing plan was for him to appeal to everyone; men, women, space aliens. Ricky Johnson wasn't trying to hide his true identity. He had no idea what that was.

Irwin felt sorry for Ricky. His work with rats had shown him what a little too much of this or that chemical could do. He pictured Ricky as a rat-man in a laboratory cage, getting an electric shock each time he approached a rat-woman, and another shock each time he approached a rat-man. The only zap-free zone was the exercise wheel, where he raced frantically while white-coated technicians cheered.

Irwin smiled encouragingly at the specimen in front of him. "Have a seat, Mr. Johnson. What can we do for you?"

"I believe I can help you fellows out." Milton winced at the high-pitched voice and crossed his legs protectively.

George had heard variations of this phrase a thousand times during his career as a policeman. "I believe I can help you out, officer." Ricky Johnson, Superstar, wanted to squeal on his friends for a price. "Please, please, Mr. Johnson, you're our guest. There's nothing you need to do for us." George hated snitches.

"Oh God, you've got to help me." Ricky fell to his knees in front of Milton's chair. Milton threw himself back into the chair, covering his crotch with his hands and upsetting the chair in the process. The chair skidded out from under him. His head met the floor with a loud crunch.

Horrified, Ricky had no idea what he had done to frighten the man with the invisible balls, but he knew he was in trouble now. "I've got millions," he yelled, knowing this declaration got him out of most uncomfortable situations.

"Judas on a Jackass!" Milt sat up, rubbed his head and looked at the crack his skull had made in the stage. "Can't you just say you're sorry?"

"Well, I don't know. I never have. I find people prefer money. Besides, my lawyers usually handle those sort of things." Ricky looked bewildered. "I haven't been out by myself since my first hit CD. What do you want me to do?"

Milton was afraid the singer was about to burst into tears. "Oh, for Christ's sake. Just say you're sorry."

"That's it? I'm sorry? And you won't sue me, or kill me? Oh yes," Ricky's face glowed in revelation, "I'm sorry. I'm so sorry. And you mean people accept this instead of money? I'm desperately and truly sorry, and…"

"And two more things," Milt interrupted the rapture.

"Yes, yes, anything. I'm so magnificently sorry. And grateful. Eternally sorry and grateful. What two things?"

"Shut the fuck up!"

"And?"

"Lose the red toenails."

CHAPTER 15
THE NAKED AND THE DENSE

Bambi shivered, naked, in the small room Irwin had led her to. Her suitcase had disappeared while she was in the shower washing away police station odors of hooker cologne and drunk-tank vomit. In its place on the bed was a pathetic little pile of garage-sale bargains obviously belonging to someone on the cleaning staff and left there in error. The bedclothes were missing, as well as the bath towels. Bambi had dabbed at herself with a hand towel and was seated on the bare mattress. She had tried sitting on the chair, but didn't like the sucking sound her buttocks made against the imitation leather when she moved. She was certain Irwin would be by any minute with her suitcase and fresh bed linen.

She had been too absorbed with martyrdom to pay much attention to what Irwin was trying to tell her on the ride back from jail. She was hoping the photographer had gotten a compelling picture of her arrest for the window of Victorianarama. At first, she'd been furious that she could not reach her attorney, or any attorney, but later decided that the unusual length of her incarceration would add to the drama of the retelling. Irwin tried to explain to her why the phone lines had been jammed, but she'd been too busy planning a solidarity speech to ex-convict sisters.

She hadn't even noticed that her fence was missing when they stopped by her house to pack for the surprise trip Irwin had planned for her. She'd been released into his custody, and she figured she had better humor him for a couple of days. She didn't ask how he knew she had been arrested. She assumed her protest had been covered on the eleven o'clock news. In reality, an exasperated desk Sergeant had called in on a pledge line to ask if Irwin happened to be related to one Bambi Schwep…and would he please come and get her before the mink-draped hookers hung her by their stoles.

MOONLIGHT BOWL MANIFESTO

CHAPTER 16

GOOD FENCES MAKE GOOD NEIGHBORS?

Margaret Mitchell came out to give Vivica a break. Veronica had been crying for twenty minutes and didn't seem to notice that the daughter handing her tissues had suddenly developed a southern accent. "There, there, tomorrow is another day," she drawled. If you had good material, use it, was Margaret's philosophy.

"But, he's left me," wailed the widow Lakeland.

"He's a freaking pig." Phanny couldn't take this whining another second. "He didn't leave her. He ran off to join the other freaking pigs. Tell her, Margaret, or I'll come out and invite her to a barbeque."

"Shut up, Phanny."

"What, Dear?"

"Nothing, Mother. As God is my witness, we'll never go hungry again!"

"Huh?"

Vivica knew it was time to take control. "Mother, we'll find him. Let's call all of the neighbors and ask if anyone has seen him."

"I don't know any of the neighbors, except Lance. They're all new since you moved away."

"Mother, that was ten years ago."

"I've been busy."

"Do you know any of their names? We could look them up in the phone book."

"Oh, I have all their names."

"Great."

"Maybe not. They're on a petition they all signed to get your father banished from the neighborhood. They said he stinks."

73

⌘⌘⌘

Serene Bright and Lance Cornell swept up glass from the shattered patio door while Harmony punched number one on the speed dial—his attorney. "All circuits are busy. Please try your call again later," a mechanical voice told him for the fifth time. He got the same results when he punched number two, his crystal therapist, and number three, 911.

"Give it a rest. The lines are clogged with people calling in pledges." Lance sucked at a small glass cut on his thumb.

"And who would you be, again?" Harmony asked.

"Well, if you live here, and I live there," Lance pointed the broom handle through the broken door toward his now visible house, "I guess that makes us neighbors. Howdy, neighbor." Lance stuck out his hand with the bleeding thumb.

"I hope you don't think I'm legally responsible for your injury," Harmony ignored the proffered hand. "I didn't invite you onto this property. As a matter of fact, you're trespassing." Harmony punched number one again.

"We must do lunch sometime," Lance told Harmony. He wiped his bloody thumb on his jeans and winked at Serene, who had crawled under the table to soothe her quaking bulldog. "I've got a pig to find," he told her.

Lance left the Brights and followed a trail of devastation from the glass-sprinkled kitchen into a living room littered with crushed and scattered furniture, through a hole in the wall next to the front door that was just the right size for a five-hundred pound mammal.

Upstairs, in Harmony's bedroom, Sherie stretched and wrinkled her surgically sculpted nose.

"Harmony," she called without leaving the down-filled warmth of Harmony's bed. "What stinks?"

CHAPTER 17
THE NAMING

Serene stood close to Harmony in line under the S banner, clutching her birth certificate. "Harmony, do you think I can be a Jessica? All my friends are Jessica."

"Not any more. And I told you to call me Daddy."

"But, Har...Daddy, can I call you by your new name? The man on TV said we had to use our new names so we could be a family." Serene pointed to the overhead monitor, where Irwin Schwep earnestly explained one of his theories.

"That's not what he said, and no, you may not call me by my new name."

"But, Daddy, you said I couldn't call you Daddy."

"That's before they stuck me with great-grandfather's name." Harmony had been dubbed "Horace" at the H window earlier that morning.

Two Easter escorts had arrived at dawn and politely herded Harmony and Serene into a white truck smelling curiously of chocolate fudge and vanilla ice cream. Under the freshly painted Latin motto on the side of the truck, the faint outline of a giant Popsicle could still be seen. The previous owner, bankrupt since the consumption of fat had been declared the eighth deadly sin, had been delighted when Leon offered him ten cents on the dollar for his fleet. Harmony was handed a clipboard and a pencil, and he and Serene were motioned to a picnic bench bolted to the bed of the truck. After the Easters helped them buckle the makeshift seatbelts Marge had insisted be installed in these vehicles, Harmony and Serene looked prepared for a picnic in tornado country. Sherie was no longer a member of the Bright household. Following instructions broadcast on television, radio and loudspeakers to "go home to your own families where you belong," she had packed up and returned to her husband. She only hoped her husband's girlfriend had gone home to her family as well.

Serene tried to look serious as she watched her father fill out the questionnaire attached to the clipboard. Terrible things were happening, he had told her—but she had never had so much fun in all of her short life. Goty chased a pig. A pig chased Goty. She met a nice neighbor who winked at her. That horrible Sherie had left after sailing across the terrazzo on a pile of pig poop. She got to ride in an ice cream truck, and—best of all—she was to stay with Harmony until the "terrible thing" was over.

Not that she didn't love her mother, but she and her mother had been living in Reno since the divorce became final, and no one was being allowed to leave California at the moment. She would miss her mom, but she wouldn't miss the acting lessons or the dance and voice classes her mother had been forcing on her since her second birthday as "a hedge against inflation." She giggled when Harmony broke the point of his pencil and the Easter escort magically pulled a new one from his nose and handed it to her dad with a flourish. With uncharacteristic docility, Harmony continued to fill out the form.

After the incident with Lance and the pig, Harmony had tried for twenty minutes to call his attorney and the police. He considered driving to his lawyer's office or the police station, but with a Hampshire-sized gap next to his front door and his fence mysteriously reduced to termite fast-food, he couldn't run the risk of looters, or narcotics agents, rummaging through his house while he was gone. Sherie had been no help. She ran

MOONLIGHT BOWL MANIFESTO

screaming and gagging to the bathroom after sliding shitshod across the kitchen floor. His hapless guard dog trembled in a cold yellow puddle under the table. The only neighbor he knew was stalking the giant pig, against which Harmony had signed a petition but had never, until today, actually seen. Harmony did the only thing he could do—he lit a joint and turned on the tube just in time to see one of the many re-runs of the previous night's announcement.

Although shocked, Harmony Bright was not a man who panicked easily. He knew the lawyers would have some sort of deal worked out soon. He recognized a negotiating ploy when he saw one on TV. If negotiations failed, California attorneys would sue the pants off these impudent bowlingbaggers and end up owning the rest of the country. By his third joint, Harmony had convinced himself that the Easter Revolution was the best thing that ever happened to California. However, the newscast that followed the re-run instantly sank his euphoric boat. His delusions of West Coast domination went up in puffs of pungent smoke.

The Easter holding the microphone smiled into the camera. *"As a part of their plan to wake up California* (The reporter had wanted to say 'shake up California' but realized that phrase might be a bit insensitive), *the Founding Four have decided to treat some of you Nates...oh, excuse me,"* the reporter squinted at the teleprompter, *"that's natives..."* But it was too late. With one more slip of the tongue, native Californians had been christened with the name of a body part usually reserved for sitting or mooning *"...have decided to treat you natives to a vacation. They are starting with lawyers."*

The scene switched to a train station. A colorful line of polyester-shirted men and women snaked from the train through

77

the terminal and out onto the sidewalk. Thousands of angry voices competed with the engine's roar for attention, but two sounds, heard over and over again, could be distinguished from the din: "Chug, chug," from the engine, and "Sue. Sue." from the line. The camera then panned the length of the one-hundred-car train, where out of almost every window a middle finger wagged. *"They sure look like they could use a good rest, don't they folks?"*

Harmony blanched and grabbed for his phone. He punched number one. This time he got a new recording, "We're sorry. The number you have reached has been temporarily disconnected." He knew then. There was no hope.

The clipboard flew from Harmony's lap when the truck came to a sudden stop. "Sorry," the Easter apologized. "Fred used to drive a cab in New York. He stops like that to shake spare change out of people's pockets." After a short time, the doors opened and three more bewildered passengers holding clipboards were ushered to seats. But, before they could be strapped in, Harmony spoke up.

"Excuse me. There's some kind of mistake here. This is our ride." The frightened newcomers backed toward the doors.

"Oh, heck no. There's no mistake. Come on in guys. Plenty of room in here." The Easter from Wisconsin patted the bench.

Harmony, who had never ridden in a bus and used an inflatable dummy to drive in the car-pool lane, tried again. "I really don't think there's enough air in here for all of us."

The Easter's smile faded and his tone hardened. "Look, Nate, this ain't a fucking limo, and you ain't the fucking King of England." All six passengers rode the rest of the way in silence.

The Naming Committee had commandeered high-school gymnasiums across the state. At the school in Harmony's neighborhood, the Pep Squad had volunteered to help hang the banners over the registration tables. Consequently, the banners weren't in strict alphabetical order, but they were close. Although most banners displayed a single letter, several names merited their own registration desks: there were separate flags for Brittanys, Jennifers and LaToyas.

When the Brights arrived, the gym was already crowded. However, Californians were conditioned to standing in long lines even before standing *in line* became standing *on line*; and, in fact, believed that if the line wasn't long, the attraction wasn't worthy. Enterprising restaurateurs were even known to hold tables back until a line had formed outside, enticing customers from the street. Next to being insulted by a snotty waiter, nothing impressed a Californian more than a long line. Theater managers held moviegoers in queues behind velvet ropes in the rain, while comfortable lobby chairs went unused. If passersby didn't see long lines, they considered the movie a flop. Harmony and Serene stood compliantly under a two-foot high H until his turn came.

"Tree and birth, please." Harmony handed the clerk his birth certificate and the genealogy chart he had filled out on the ride over. After glancing at the documents, the clerk typed for a few seconds on her keyboard, then stood and extended her hand to Harmony. "Nice to meet you, Horace." Still holding his hand, she pulled him closer to her and fastened an armband with Velcro between his elbow and his shoulder. "If you're seen without this armband, we'll warn you once. The second infraction, you get a tattoo on your forehead. Watch the video. Have a nice day." She pulled his new birth certificate from the printer and handed it to him. "Don't forget your family tree. You'll need it for your daughter."

When she finally stood in front of the S table, Serene suddenly became shy.

"Do you have your papers, Sweetheart?" the S lady coaxed.

"Do I have to change my name to be a family?"

"Do you know where your name came from, Sweetie?" The clerk gently pried the record of her delivery from Serene's sticky hands and noticed that the place of birth had been listed as Under Water, California.

"Mother's psychic saw it in a vision." The clerk sighed and reached for the chart Harmony held out to her.

"Do you know your great-grandmother's name?" Serene shook her head, worried that she had failed some kind of a test. "Your grandmother?" Again a negative reply. "Do you know why we are giving you a new name?" Negative. *"Doesn't anybody watch the video?"* wondered the clerk.

⌘⌘⌘

Lance and Veronica watched Irwin Schwep on the monitor strapped to the basketball hoop. "…and if you are named after a parent, grandparent, or great-grandparent…" Irwin explained from the screen, "…you are much more likely to feel a connection with that person…"

Lance absently scratched the rash that began and ended where his new Murphy's Bar and Grill Pin Busters shirt covered his body. He and Veronica had already received their armbands, and Veronica had been renamed Velma, after her maternal grandmother. Lance had been dubbed Lancelot Cornell III at birth, and so was allowed to keep his father's and grandfather's name. The other members of their van pool were still in the trendy *J* line, so Lance and Velma/Veronica were killing time finding fault with Irwin's appearance as he continued his speech.

"…are more likely to feel that person is a part of you. You

are a continuation of that person."

"And he's a continuation of bad taste," Velma/Veronica offered.

"Come on, Vee (the naming committee was allowing nicknames and a grateful Velma had jumped on 'Vee' when Lance suggested it), you can do better than that. Look at his hair...it looks like the ends were chewed off by a raccoon."

"It's hard to make fun of someone who is dressed exactly like you." Vee defended her dulled rapier wit. "And, anyway, this is Vivica's game, not mine. I think this guy has some interesting things to say." Vee turned her attention back to the screen.

"How would it feel to see your own name printed on papers committing a parent to a nursing home? Damned odd, I'm telling you. Damned odd." Irwin paused for what he hoped would be dramatic effect. "Would you be seeing your own future? Makes you think, doesn't it?"

"Makes me think he's damned odd." Lance improvised a comedian's drum roll with his fingers against a wastepaper basket and handed the barb off to Vee. She ignored him. The image hovering above the basketball hoop held her attention. "Damn," Lance muttered. "I wish Viv were here."

"Ethel, Ethel, Ethel." Serene sang her new name as her finger traced the bright yellow smiley face stitched onto her black armband. "Daddy, do I really have a grandmother Ethel?"

"A great-grandmother."

"Where is she? Can I visit her?"

"She lives in a special place for old people, called Florida. It's too far away to visit."

"But, Daddy, I have to know her. I have to make sure she's all right."

"Why?"

"I have her name."

⌘⌘⌘

Vivica had been hiding at Lance's house since "the rattlesnake round-up," as the deportation of all lawyers from the state had become popularly known. She hadn't practiced law since her fourth husband sued her second husband for non-support of his first wife who also happened to be her fourth husband's third wife. After her summation to the jury which ended "Ladies and gentlemen, this sucks," Vivica sued her husband for divorce on the grounds of mental cruelty, and was awarded his mansion and enough alimony to keep her comfortably idle 'til death do her part. She wasn't taking any chances, however, and decided discretion was the better part of not ending up on a train bound for hell—or so rumor had its destination. Phanny and Margaret were not so eager to remain underground.

"*This is the dawning of the Age of Aquarius*," sang Phanny.

"This is extortion, plain and simple," put in Vivica.

"But, they don't want anything," said Phanny. "Don't you get it? They're trying to save us from ourselves. 'Oh, brave new world, that has such people in't!'"

"The land! The land! We can't let them take Tara." Margaret Mitchell looked out Lance's back window at the combined yards of the neighborhood, no longer divided into selfish, frightened little territories by fences, but looking, instead, like one large, bountiful estate.

Phanny pinched herself to get Margaret's attention. "They're not taking our land away, you delusional redneck. They're trying to give it back to us."

CHAPTER 18

ROOTS

Ricky's bare toes, sans polish, wiggled themselves free of the superfluous blanket in which he tucked them, and the rest of his body, each night. Most of the sleepers used no covers at all, nor even wore pajamas. The cot-filled room was warmed by Santa Ana winds and by hundreds of snorers exhaling body-heated breath. The air conditioner was set at minimum cooling because, as Marge put it, "We don't own stock in PG&E." Had he been aware of his own substantial holdings however, Ricky could have argued that he did, indeed, own stock in Pacific Gas and Electric. He felt protected under his thin wool wall. If he pulled the cover over his head, he didn't have to see the powerful, professionally sculpted bodies all around him; and they couldn't see his boyishly soft one.

A trickle of sweat down the back of his neck tickled Ricky as he slept. During the night, his constant tossing had freed one end of his turban, which snagged on a corner of the bed and unwound as Ricky pitched and rolled restlessly in fretful sleep. While he dreamed prophetically of Isadora Duncan, the cloth formerly coiled around his head, twisted around his neck, tighter and tighter with every restless turn. At the very moment the dream Isadora was strangled by her own scarf, Ricky's contortions to blot the sweat from his neck with his pillow cinched the material at his throat into a garrote. With strangulation imminent, he awoke, clawing at the noose around his neck. With each frantic thrust of his body, the turban cut deeper into his windpipe.

"Jumping John the Baptist! Are you trying to decapitate

yourself?" Milton placed a restraining knee on the suffocating superstar's chest. "Take it easy." More calmly than he felt, Milt slashed at the offending fabric with his Swiss Army knife until a desperate sucking sound followed by short gasps told him that Ricky was breathing again. Ricky's head lolled against the pillow like a bobbing dog ornament in the back window of a Chevy.

"Don't try to talk." Milt ordered Ricky. "Go back to sleep. We'll discuss this in the morning." Milt gathered the shredded pieces of headdress and stuffed them into his pocket for disposal later. As he continued his rounds as dorm monitor, a poem he was forced to memorize in high school ran through his head:

> *Though I've belted you and flayed you,*
> *By the livin' Gawd that made you,*
> *You're a better man than I am, Gunga Din.*

"Bullshit," said Milt to himself.

Afraid to lift his head for fear it would fall off, Ricky lay in darkness softly stroking his bruised throat. His hair, freed from the turban, fanned out in stiff spikes around his pillowed head like the crown on the Statue of Liberty; bits of white fiber fluff clung like barnacles to the bristly ends. One delicate hand drifted to his jawline to scratch a sweat itch and encountered, instead of moisture, something prickly. Unsuccessfully, he tried to brush the foreign object from his face. He scraped the spot with a fingernail; still, a tiny spear pricked his finger—dozens of tiny spears assaulted his fingertips.

He panicked. *"Bedbugs!"* An acidy fluid rose from his stomach, burned his sore throat and filled his mouth. Suddenly, from somewhere deep in his hormone-stifled body, a genetic memory emerged triumphant at last and Ricky knew. Bedbugs, shit—these were whiskers! Deprived by his captors of any hormone treatments or chemical injections, Ricky Johnson was finally, at age thirty-eight, going through puberty.

⌘⌘⌘

The thick black line down the center of Marguerite's scalp reminded Chelsea of a shampoo ad she had once seen comparing two types of dandruff shampoo. "*Natural blonde, my ass,*" she thought as she stood next to Marguerite at the long locker-room mirror. Chelsea's own hair had been dyed back to its natural chestnut color for a recent movie, and consequently she wasn't suffering the same growing-out pains as most of the female population, and many of the male population of the Center were. She had even been pleasantly surprised to discover that shampoo purchased by the gallon cleaned just as well as the hundred-dollar-an-ounce placenta extract formula she used at home.

"Hey, Fatso, if you tug on your ears, does your head pull apart?" Chelsea asked Marguerite's reflection.

"Oh, is somebody there? I thought it was just a crack in the mirror." Marguerite elbowed the emaciated actress into the hand dryer mounted to the wall and peered fretfully at her image. "I'm starting to look like one of those women waiting in line at Graceland." As she raked her fingers through her hair, she snagged a fingernail and tore it off at the quick. "Fupf," she said, sucking on the injured digit.

"For starters, don't part it in the middle." Chelsea ignored the body slam, figuring God had evened the score with the fingernail. "That only emphasizes the roots. Can't you kind of poof it up all over?"

"Without gel, or mousse, or hairspray, or a hairdresser?"

"At least your hair is growing out dark, not gray. Half the people here would sell their souls—or at least their agent's souls—for a tube of Grecian Formula. Relax. The only cameras allowed around here are the ones Irwin uses to tape his inspirational messages or to broadcast to the masses. Big Brother with a gut. Except he's not really watching us, he's watching himself. Come on. I've got an idea."

⌘⌘⌘

"Good morning, Alice. How about some of your lovely slime-green Jell-O." Marguerite slapped her tray onto the counter rail.

"Is today green day, Dear?" The cafeteria ladies had grown accustomed to Marguerite's little eccentricities, and if they didn't break the rules, allowed for them. "I thought you didn't like our Jell-O."

"Whatever gave you that idea?"

"I don't know, Dear. Maybe the fact that you called it 'boogers in a bowl' and threw it across the room."

"It did stick to the wall pretty good, didn't it?" Marguerite grinned in apology.

"I'm afraid we don't serve Jell-O for breakfast."

Marguerite leaned across steaming bowls of oatmeal and whispered to Alice, "Confidentially, it's for 'the stick.'" She jerked her chin toward Chelsea, who sat at a table with nothing in front of her but a glass of water. "She told me she loves the crap. Maybe I can get her to eat something."

"Oh, of course. I think we have some in the kitchen. Let

me check." Alice, who believed all of Chelsea Dove's much publicized tantrums were caused by poor nutrition, scurried to the kitchen and returned almost immediately, balancing a transparent, glutinous mountain that lurched from side to side as she walked. "Is this enough?"

⌘⌘⌘

Chelsea had vacated her mother's womb after only a seven-month's stay. Had she known in advance there would be a cheering, applauding mob of people surrounding her mother's cervix when she made her entrance into the world through the hairy curtain, she might have chosen to stay in for an extra two months and rehearse her lines. She did, however, cry right on cue when the midwife slapped her wee behind. At five pounds, no ounces, she was immediately labeled "tiny and cute" by the twenty-five people living with her parents on a commune in Big Sur.

The first time she stopped eating, Chelsea was six years old. Anorexia was not as yet a popular talk show topic, and because she was normally such a good girl, her mother assumed her self-imposed starvation was only a phase. After her perfect little daughter went three weeks without eating, Chelsea's mother left the commune, against her husband's wishes, to take her only child to a real doctor for the first time in her life. The pediatrician found nothing physically wrong with Chelsea, but asked to speak to her alone.

"If you don't eat, you won't grow up big and strong."

"Yes, I know." The bright-eyed moppet looked directly into the doctor's eyes.

"But don't you want to grow up someday?"

"No thank you. Big people are bad. Only children are

nice."

The doctor clenched his fist and wondered what this beautiful child had seen to make her so afraid of adults. "Did some big person hurt you?"

"Oh, no. Big people are very nice to children. They're only mean to each other. So I'll just stay little."

"But, Sweetie, if you don't eat, you'll die."

"If I only eat a tiny bit, can I stay little?"

"I'm sorry, but it doesn't work that way. You don't want your mother to be sad do you?"

With those words, Chelsea sighed, and at age six, assumed the responsibility of her mother's happiness. If her father couldn't make her mother happy, she would have to. Chelsea always did what was right. She was a perfect little girl.

⌘⌘⌘

"Look, Slats, who's this?" Marguerite turned away briefly. When she spun back to face Chelsea, she grabbed her stomach, made exaggerated retching noises, and spewed lime Jell-O from her mouth and nose. "It's you…after a big meal."

"You have as much class as your sitcom. Do you want me to help you or not?"

"Okay, okay. My hair's not going to turn green or draw flies, is it?"

Chelsea worked the substitute mousse into a liquid in the palms of her hands, applied it to the hefty actress's hair, and then used her fingers to plump and rearrange it until Marguerite's dark secrets were no longer visible. "It'll be a little stiff when it dries."

"It looks great." The two women jumped at the sound of a bass voice rumbling out of nowhere. "I didn't mean to scare you." This time the voice squeaked out the last two words as a man stepped from behind an enormous pile of laundry. "I didn't want anyone to see me."

"Well, Ricky J., you little pixie. Is that you? What the hell happened? What's wrong with your voice?" Marguerite had never met Ricky, few people had. She almost didn't recognize him without his heavy makeup and outlandish costumes, and the fact that dryer lint had been added to the debris clinging to the bristles on top of his head.

"I've been hiding in here since the night shift left. Can you help?" Ricky pointed to his hair. He was about to offer money, but remembered the lesson he had learned from Milt. "I'd be forever grateful."

"Yeah, so who the fuck cares about your gratitude? Let's talk about the leading female role in your next movie."

Ricky was back on ground he could walk on. "It's yours. Have your agent call my people."

"Where's your turban?" Chelsea asked.

Ricky's hand flew involuntarily to his throat. "It's a long story. Just help me get to the barbershop. They haven't got a stylist, but maybe they have a scissors I can stab myself in the heart with."

The three of them looked around the laundry room for something to hide Ricky's hair until they could get him to the Easter's barber shop. The towels and sheets had already been laundered by the night crew of Nates and delivered before dawn to the shower rooms and dormitories. The day crew was in charge of clothing.

"I think I've found something." Chelsea waved a can of spray starch.

The three Nates walked through the long corridors

together. The big blonde looked anxiously into every reflecting surface they passed for evidence of hair-shaft betrayal or insect infestation. The thin one licked dried gelatin from her knuckles. The young man of indeterminate ethnicity prayed that his heavily lacquered coif would maintain its smooth, slicked-back appearance until they reached the barbershop. Each time he patted his head for reassurance, a lock of stiffened, over-processed, tortured hair broke off, leaving a trail of hairy spoor to be puzzled over later by the cleaning crew.

"You've really got to do something about that cold, Ricky," Marguerite commented as they walked. "You could lose your voice."

"I don't think it's a cold," he answered proudly in sonorous tones. "And, by the way, call me Rick."

MOONLIGHT BOWL MANIFESTO

CHAPTER 19

THE VISIT

Marge and the kids waved the bus down at a stop two blocks from the Center, near the exit of the secret tunnel built so superstars could "pull an Elvis" on their suffocating fans. Lenore proudly deposited exact change in the fare box and she and Marge found a seat together. Leonard glared menacingly at a seat-hogging Nate until he made room for Leonard to sit. Leonard grinned his appreciation. Besides the instructor, they were the only Easters on the bus. The rest of the passengers wore black and yellow armbands and expressions of terror mixed with disdain, as if they were about to be hanged with an off-brand rope. They were learning how to take the bus.

The instructor consulted his clipboard and pointed at the Nate sitting next to Leonard. "All right. You're next. Your stop is two blocks away. What do you do?"

The Nate rapidly flipped the pages of the pamphlet on his lap. "I press the bar and carefully move to my nearest exit."

"That's great. Except for one thing. While you were reading, we passed your stop. But, press the bar anyway, and go to the next stop."

Juan Escobar, the driver of the training bus, watched his rear-view mirror with amusement as the man caromed from side to side of the rolling bus, grabbing seat backs and other passengers for support. Juan pulled slowly into the loading zone, swooshed the heavy doors open and waited for the man to exit.

"I'm afraid you'll have to turn around. I've missed my stop," the Nate ordered the driver.

"Chu hab a nice day." Juan used one of the two phrases he knew in English. He glanced significantly at the open door in case his meaning hadn't seeped through.

"No, you don't understand. You've gone too far."

"Hexact chanz only." Juan was getting nervous, and used the only other English he knew. He jerked his chin toward the exit and winked at the uncomprehending passenger.

Indignant murmuring circulated through the pleasantly conditioned air of the bus. "...probably an illegal...pay his salary..damned beaner. Of all the nerve...turn this bus around this second or...bet he has a knife..." Juan didn't understand what they were saying, but suspected their anger was directed at him. He looked to the instructor for assistance.

"Get off the bus." The man started at the instructor's order. The murmuring ceased.

"But, he missed my stop."

"*You* missed your stop. This bus goes in one direction... forward. Get off the bus."

"But how will I get back?"

"Walk."

A collective gasp from the passengers made Juan's colon tighten. "Walk back to your stop, cross the street and wait for the eastbound bus to take you back to our meeting point. Wait for us. When we're all back, we'll have pizza and beer. We've been over this before. Doesn't anybody watch the videos?"

As Juan pulled away from the curb, forty native Californians watched from the windows as their brother Nate grew smaller and smaller in the distance. They were sure they would never see him again. If only they had gotten his name...

MOONLIGHT BOWL MANIFESTO

⌘⌘⌘

Marge rang the doorbell again. She could hear a dog barking inside, and she thought she heard someone moving around. The visits had been her idea, and she wasn't going to give up easily. She knocked. The walk from the bus stop had been long, but her legs were sturdy and the children helped her carry her packages. Marge remembered the house from her many drives through the neighborhood, when she and the kids would pretend they had a home there. It was the only house on the block without an alarm company sign on the front lawn, and Marge was hoping it might contain people like herself, with nothing much to protect from burglars. On her arrival, she had been a little disappointed to discover a Brinks Security sign hidden behind an overgrown shrub. A huge patch of mismatched fresh stucco on the wall next to the front door made her wonder if the house had been broken into.

"Daddy, are you expecting a FedEx?" Ethel/Serene had not been allowed to play outside since the fences had come down.

"Quiet," Horace/Harmony hushed his daughter. "Whoever it is will go away."

"Look, Daddy." Ethel/Serene pointed to the unbroken side of the sliding patio doors. The other side had been covered up with cardboard taped into place. Goty snuffled his nose against the inside of the glass and wagged his stub. Two children, with their noses pressed to the outside of the glass, looked in. The doorbell rang again.

"I hope it's the police looking for these two." The two Lefkowitz children made faces at Ethel/Serene through the dog-snot covered glass. "I'll see who it is. Don't let them in," Horace/Harmony told his daughter.

"Good morning," Marge greeted Horace when he yanked open the front door. "I was in the neighborhood, and I thought I would drop in."

"Who the hell are you? Are those your brats trespassing on my property?"

This was not what was supposed to happen. Marge burst into tears. "I've brought cookies." She held out a basket covered in pink cellophane and tied with a white bow.

"Oh, jeez, come in for a minute. But I'm not buying any cookies."

"So you see," Marge explained to Horace/Harmony and Ethel/Serene as they perched nervously on the edge of the sofa cushions, "the way I was raised, friends drop in on friends and people welcome people to the neighborhood."

"But, I don't know you."

"Well, Irwin believes you can never have too many friends."

"Irwin?"

"The videos, Daddy." Ethel/Serene hovered like a curious humming bird.

"Oh." Horace/Harmony twitched. He had absolutely no idea what to do with a guest. If he had to meet people socially, he met them at a bar or a club. If he brought someone to his house, it was usually for sex.

"Would you like to try a cookie? They're homemade," Marge offered.

He took the cookie the strange woman held out and set it on the end table next to him. A wet, wrinkled muzzle appeared from behind the table, and a rough tongue swept the cookie into Goty's mouth. Horace/Harmony did not appear to notice. "So, do you think you're going to be here for a while?" Horace/Harmony asked.

"Well, if you don't mind. It was a long bus trip. I think your little girl would enjoy having someone to play with."

"It could get kind of noisy in here with three kids running around."

"Let them play outside, with the dog."

"I don't think it's safe, without a fence."

"Don't be silly. Your yard is beautiful, with its pool and its orange trees."

"We don't have a pool, or orange trees. They belong to other houses. We have a Zen garden and avocado trees."

"But you can see them, and share the beauty, and smell the blossoms. Please let the children play outside."

"Maybe. I'll be right back." Horace/Harmony went to the desk in his den and rummaged through several drawers. After finding what he was looking for, he returned to his guest and handed her a card.

"You'll have to sign this," he told her.

On the front of the card was a brightly colored circus clown holding a balloon that read "Come to my party!" The inside held the usual spaces for place, time, host and RSVP information.

"I don't understand. Are you having a birthday party?"

"No. Turn it over. You have to sign the back."

Marge turned the card over. The back of the card was a liability waiver, freeing the host from financial responsibility for any injuries received on his/her property resulting from attendance at or transportation to and from any function held on such property or any visit to such property. Marge knew exactly what she wanted to do with the card, but, after looking at three small, hopeful faces, she sighed and signed. Horace/Harmony retrieved the disclaimer and stuffed it in his back pocket.

Leonard skipped another rock across the smooth surface of the swimming pool. The polished, round stones he had found in Mr. Bright's yard made great skimmers. He had grown tired of the girl's chatter.

"So what, 'zactly, is a therapist?" Lenore had been frightened by Ethel/Serene's talk of seeing a doctor every single week.

"It's not like a regular doctor. No shots or anything. It's just a person you can tell all your secrets to—and she won't tell your parents."

"Oh. I have a therapist, too. Only I don't call her Doctor. I call her Grandma."

After his visitors left, and still feeling uncomfortable from the extended hug and little pat on the behind Marge had given him at the door, Horace/Harmony opened the gift she and the children had left with them. It was a cross-stitched sampler in a frame:

> *Be Not Forgetful To*
> *Entertain Strangers,*
> *For Thereby Some Have*
> *Entertained Angels*
> *Unawares.*

"Leonard Lefkowitz, what's that smell?" Marge and the children waited for the eastbound bus.

"I'm sorry, Mommy. I think I stepped in something." Embarrassed, Leonard fondled the pile of smooth stones he had stashed in his pocket. He didn't consider it stealing. They were only rocks.

"Don't worry, Sweetie. We can scrape it off." She reached into her purse. "I've just the thing." The brightly colored clown continued to smile as Mrs. Lefkowitz used his face to clean her son's shoes.

CHAPTER 20

COLD BUTT, WARM HEART

Marguerite rode Lois Lefkowitz on her left hip as she barreled through the corridor on her way to the gymnasium. Marge had deemed three-year-old Lois too young and fidgety for visiting and left her in the care of America's cantankerous, but loving, sitcom mom. Although Marge realized Marguerite was only acting the part of a capable mother every Thursday night (and in syndication almost every other night), she believed the affection shown by the actress for the children on her show could not be feigned. Six Emmy awards for best actress should have tipped her off. Marge didn't know that after each saccharin scene, whichever two-year-old twin (Mad Dog or The Crusher, as they were known by the crew) Marguerite had been working with was handed off to a baby wrangler for de-drooling and diaper inspection. The three older children on the set were sent to their trailers for therapy sessions. Marge was confident, if misguided, that her baby would be well cared for.

Marguerite had been afraid to turn down the babysitting request. This was, after all, the Hunk's spawn, and there could be retribution if she refused. She tried to foist the little tit-sucker off on Chelsea, but the child wanted nothing to do with her blade-hipped, hard-ribbed body and screamed every time Chelsea came near her. She preferred to cuddle against the soft folds and interesting crevices of Marguerite's comforting corporeal mass. She spent the day attached like a tumor to Marguerite's body.

When Marguerite stopped momentarily to rub some

circulation back into her numbed left arm, she saw a dressing room door open a crack and heard a plaintive voice call, "Help me, please."

"Who's talking to me? Ricky, is that you? Your new voice crap out on you?" Marguerite instinctively hugged Lois closer.

"Please, come in." The door opened enough for Marguerite to see the occupant.

"Well, okay, I guess. I can see you're not armed." Marguerite stepped cautiously into the room and Bambi quickly closed the door behind her. "Somebody steal your clothes?"

"Yes, my husband."

"So, what are those?" Maguerite pointed to a shirt, jeans, panties and bra hanging over the back of a chair.

"I refuse to wear them. I'm protesting." Bambi shivered. Irwin had adjusted the thermostat in the room to encourage her cooperation.

"Protesting, hell. You're freezing. Your nipples are standing at attention. Do you expect me to salute? At least put on some underwear. There's a kid here, for Christ's sake."

From her lower vantage, Lois could see fading half-moon scars under Bambi's breasts. "Oooh! Owie," she pointed.

Bambi grabbed the bra, knocking over the chair in her haste to hide her secret. Jane Fonda couldn't solve all figure problems. She fastened the hook in back and settled each expensive breast into its own cup before pulling the straps up over her shoulders. She stepped into the sensible cotton underpants Marge had purchased by the gross, and threw herself down dramatically on the bare mattress. "I'm a prisoner here," she whined.

"So? Welcome to the club. At least you've got this room

and a private bath. You think you've got scars? Try showering with fifteen hundred celebrities. You'll see more stitches than on an AIDS quilt."

"You don't understand. I can't leave this room."

"You let me in. The door isn't locked. What's your problem?"

"I can't be seen in these clothes."

"Look, lady, I don't have time for this shit now. I've got to get this kid to her father by three o'clock." Bambi didn't know that Lois was the daughter of one of her husband's best friends and co-revolutionary. She had never bothered to learn if any of his friends had families.

"If you want my advice," Marguerite said as she opened the door, "just put on the fucking jeans, and the fucking shirt, and get on with your fucking life."

⌘⌘⌘

Irwin and George were shirts, Leon and Milt were skins. Holding a real basketball in his hands felt good to Milton, but scoring points had been easier with an invisible ball. "Time out," he called, when he saw Marguerite enter the gym with his tiny daughter. Gratefully, Irwin and George collapsed against a pile of blue jeans and mopped their faces with Milt's and Leon's cast-off shirts. They had been playing half court. The rest of the gymnasium was filled with jeans and an ever-increasing supply of bowling shirts. Apparently, the Easters had tapped into a bottomless well of polyester when they requested donations; however, Irwin had to ask several times on national television for people to stop sending old bowling trophies along with the shirts.

"Daddy, Daddy!" Lois held out her chubby arms to her

father.

"How's my little pumpkin? Did you have a good time with the nice lady?"

Marguerite held her breath. She'd given the kid everything she'd asked for all day, including two hotdogs at lunch. Luckily, she'd already thrown those up.

"Yes, Daddy. Fun." She patted her dad's bare chest and wrinkled her nose. She didn't like the way he smelled after he played games with his friends. "Daddy."

"What, Pumpkin Puss?"

"Put your fucking shirt on."

Marguerite was out of the door and hiding in the laundry room before her footsteps stopped echoing in the gym.

CHAPTER 21

ALL DOGS GO TO HEAVEN

The dogs were usually old, and often smelled of decayed teeth, rotted by sweet treats fed lovingly by gnarled and spotted hands.

The man had tried, in the beginning, to find homes for all of them, but no one wanted old dogs either. He had seen the first one, a poodle, licking the tears from an old lady's face on the eleven o'clock news. The scene made a great program teaser, and had been played at every commercial break that evening. The old lady had entrusted her son with her power of attorney. Her son had responded by using that power to evict the septuagenarian from her tiny home.

When interviewed, her son's lawyer explained that the property had been sold for her benefit, and she would be taken care of in an elder care facility for the rest of her life. He did not add that her son would also be taken care of, on an island in the Caribbean, for the rest of his life. When asked for her comment, the old woman could only cry and hug her dog. She would be cared *for*, but not cared *about*...homes for the aged did not allow pets. The man remembered his own dog, Rusty, and called the television station.

⌘⌘⌘

Rusty and his master retired together and headed out west. They had been partners for eight years. The man drove and Rusty rode shotgun with his head out the window, tongue lolling and ears flapping in the wind. Every fifty miles or so,

Rusty wiggled under the steering wheel onto his man's lap, and slobbered on his neck to let him know how happy he was they were together. At rest stops, Rusty chased blowing candy wrappers while his master consulted maps. For ten days they meandered across the country, enjoying new sights and smells, and each other's company. Then they reached California.

Rusty bounded joyously across the manicured sod when he saw the ducks in the pond at Marina de la Playa Luxury Apartments. They looked exactly like the ducks he had befriended at the Lincoln Park Lagoon back in Chicago. He barked a greeting. He was confused when his owner grabbed his collar, snapped a leash to it and led him back to the car.

Master and dog drove around for two days, from apartment complex to apartment complex. As the man spoke to each leasing agent, he grew angrier and sadder. Rusty was kept in the car on those stops. He knew something was wrong, and nuzzled his head against his master to comfort him. On the third day, they spent the whole day at the beach, playing fetch, eating hotdogs and splashing in the waves. The salty water tasted wonderful to the excited dog, better than Lake Michigan. That evening, the man sneaked Rusty into his room at the motel, patted a spot on the bed next to him, and spent the night sleeping with his arm around his best friend.

The next morning, the man took Rusty to the address given to him by the apartment manager two days earlier.

"They'll find a good home for him," the manager had told him. "You'll never find anyone around here who'll rent to someone with a pet. They don't have to. There's too much competition for space. No kids, either. At least you can get rid of a dog."

As the man entered the Blessed Angel Animal Haven,

MOONLIGHT BOWL MANIFESTO

he saw a purple-haired young man carry a frantic white Persian cat away through double swinging doors at the far side of the reception area. "Come on, Puff, let me show you the way." The boy seemed gentle.

Rusty began to tremble. Something was wrong. Disturbing odors filled the building. He wedged himself between his master's legs.

"You've got to know. He's a good dog. The best. It's just that I have to live near the medical center for treatment. I was wounded. It'll take six months, they said. He's trained. You'll probably want to take him home yourself. Would you? I'd give you money for food. I'd visit him."

The receptionist let him prattle on. There was nothing she could say to comfort him. She rang a bell and the attendant returned through the swinging doors. He took the leash, but the terrified Rusty braced his paws and wouldn't budge.

"Good boy, good Rusty. Go with him," the man commanded.

Always obedient, Rusty obeyed.

"Come on, Puff, I'll show you the way," the purple-haired boy said once again.

George sat behind the wheel of his car for thirty minutes, not moving, taking deep breaths and trying not to cry. *At least they could get his name right.* He decided to go back into the building. They'd live in the car if George couldn't find a place to take them both.

"Excuse me. I was just here. The attendant —he called my dog Puff. I think he has him mixed up with the cat."

The receptionist was startled. "Oh, I'm sorry. He calls all our animals Puff. It's his little joke."

"Joke?"

"Yes. Puff! Get it?"
"No."
"We're a crematorium."

⌘⌘⌘

The woman held both of George's hands tightly. "And you promise you'll find a good home for Pom-Pom?" Her rheumy old eyes searched George's for any hint of deceit. "She's such a good dog."

"Yes Ma'am." George leaned forward and kissed the wrinkled cheek.

"And she can bring her toys?"

"Of course."

"And pictures. They'll send me pictures. Her new family?"

"I'll see what I can do." George hadn't thought about documentation, but he would figure something out. He'd been haunted by the face seen on the eleven o'clock news, and couldn't bear the thought of seeing that look of desolation again.

"You're such a good boy. I wish I had a son like you."

⌘⌘⌘

Pom-Pom had been the hardest. Luckily, the poodle grieved silently, and the apartment manager never discovered she was there. He tried to find her a home. He made phone calls, placed ads and tacked up cards in grocery stores and Laundromats. After two unsuccessful weeks, George had her groomed and shot several rolls of film, posing her in Santa hats, next to Easter baskets, in the park, and with new dog toys. He waited two more days to be sure the pictures turned out before he took her to the vet.

MOONLIGHT BOWL MANIFESTO

He had given her a tranquilizer, and she was more curious than frightened when they arrived at Dr. Casey's office. George held her head and stroked her muzzle as the doctor pushed the needle in her vein. He felt her head grow heavy with death. "Good bye, ol' girl. Say hello to Rusty for me. And tell him I'm sorry."

⌘⌘⌘

"Hey, boys and girls! What time is it?" George burst through the door at the Golden Slope Retirement Home.

"It's Howdy Doody Time!" several seniors returned.

"You're absodoodily right. And I've got pictures. Look, here's Pom-Pom." George handed a picture to his old friend. "And isn't she looking perky? And, look, Jake, here's Bowzer." He gave the old man a snapshot of a bull terrier wearing a tiara and carrying a jack-o'-lantern in his mouth. "And there's more!" He fanned a dozen photos across a card table like a Las Vegas blackjack dealer. The seniors shuffled closer. Many of them smiled for the first time in weeks.

BARBARA JONES

CHAPTER 22

TRAVELERS

The room was filled with travelers. Some of them traveled to foreign lands, visiting all of the places they had read about, and may even have planned to visit earlier in their lives, had not life interfered. Most of them only traveled to a better time, when they were young and strong and loved. They traveled from wheel chairs, a palsied hand frozen in one lap, another hand trembling uncontrollably, protesting the interaction of too many drugs. A few, those who had been there the longest and were no longer strapped into wheel chairs for the semblance of care, traveled from their beds to places so dark and far away they could only be called back by God.

"They're off again…the nodders." The attendant was dressed in a white smock designed to give the impression to visitors that he might have been trained to do something. "Why don't they just shoot them?"

"It's the creepers gets me. That sound their slippers make against the linoleum. Like chalk on a blackboard, only slower." The two staff members talked over the heads of the old people as if they weren't in the room. "By the way, you owe me fifty bucks."

"Shit. Who went?"

"Room twenty seven."

"Twenty seven? He wasn't even sick."

"Yeah, that's why he was a long shot. He's been stashing meds."

"Sure you didn't help him out?"

"For fifty clams? I don't think so. Anyway, he left a

note. Said 'Fuck you.'"

The old man looked at his watch and reached under his lap robe for the paper cup hidden between his legs. It had been difficult, with his shaking hands and prostate trouble, but he had managed to fill it to the brim. He knew the two young men would soon pass him as they made their way to the patio to share the joint they stole every day from a glaucoma patient. As he heard them approach, he threw the contents of the cup in their path and faked a coughing spell to distract them. His coughing covered suppressed laughter as he watched them hydroplane across the puddle of urine, sail into the air and land on their backs in the malodorous liquid.

Little piss ants! Betting on death. How's it feel to lie in pee while someone makes fun of you?

⌘⌘⌘

"They can't leave. They need medication, skilled caretakers..." the administrator of Golden Slope argued with George.

"I think they've had more than enough medication. Half of them don't even have medical problems, yet you're drugging them into oblivion. And skilled care? That's a joke. You pay minimum wage plus anything your employees can steal from the residents."

"I won't allow them to go."

"You're forgetting who's in charge now." George didn't like to throw his weight around, but if ever a place needed liberating, this was it. "We're leaving."

"You won't get any Medicaid funds. I'll see to that. You'll kill them. You'll kill them all."

MOONLIGHT BOWL MANIFESTO

⌘⌘⌘

"Hey, boys and girls, what time is it?" George gave his usual greeting.

"It's Howdy Doody time," answered only a few faithful voices. During the two years he had been visiting the retirement home, George had watched with dismay as funding was cut for anything that might bring cheer into these peoples' lives. Bus lines no longer offered free transportation for field trips for fear of lawsuits from families should an elderly loved one be injured in an accident; although prior to an accident, families often had to be reminded that an elderly loved one existed. Restaurants no longer offered senior citizen discounts, from concern about discrimination suits. Each visit, George found more and more residents unresponsive to his greeting. They had gone traveling.

"Where is she?" George asked when Pom-Pom's mistress did not come over to say hello.

"I think she's in 1945, celebrating VE day." A resident pointed across the large day room to a woman staring vacantly into space and slowly moving her right hand as if waving a tiny flag.

George pulled a chair close enough to her for their knees to touch. He put a hand on each of her shoulders as she continued to wave the flag. He had to get her to focus. He shook her. Her right hand relaxed its grip and her head fell to her chest. She didn't want to come back. He shook her again.

"Is it Howdy Doody time again?"

George smiled in relief at the tissue-paper-wrapped sound of her voice. He knew she would be confused for a while, but the longer she talked, the longer she stayed connected with the real world, the clearer her thoughts would become—until he left again, and her world reverted to medication and Wheel Of Fortune. This time he wasn't leaving her behind.

"I've got a surprise for you," he announced to the room.

"Not another stinking magician, I hope," a surly voice challenged. Not all of the seniors were drugged into oblivion. Some were still conscious enough to be miserable. Irwin had a theory, George remembered, that God made old people crabby on purpose, so when they died, we wouldn't miss them so much.

"No, no magician." A nearby magic school sometimes sent students over to entertain, believing that old people were easier to fool. "We're blowin' this pop stand."

"Where are we going?"

"Who the hell cares. Where's the bus?"

George held up his hands for quiet. "We're going home."

⌘⌘⌘

Lance could not get rid of his rash. His doctor prescribed cortisone without success, dubbed the cause stress, and gave up.

"My hypnotherapist could clear that right up."

"I'm not possessed, Viv, I'm poisoned. It's the shirt." Lance billowed his unbuttoned shirt away from his body, getting some relief from the fanned air. "I take it off to go to sleep, the rash goes. I put it on in the morning, the rash comes back."

"So don't wear the shirt in the house."

"They've got spies everywhere, Viv. There's two Easters for every five Nates."

"What would they do if they caught you?"

"Remember the Rattlesnake Roundup?"

"You've got a point there." Vivica was sensitive about her missing brothers of the bar and had ridden the short distance from her mother's house to Lance's in the trunk of her mother's car.

Phanny believed air pollution caused Lance's skin irritation. Margaret Mitchell was just as sure that it was one of those diseases that gentle women don't talk about in mixed company; although she wasn't sure if Lance counted as mixed company. She didn't disapprove of Lance, and found him rather charming, in a sisterly sort of way. She was appalled, however, when Phanny suggested that Ashley Wilkes had really been one of "those kinds of men" and had only married the spindly Melanie because she repulsed him less than the voluptuous Scarlett.

Lance and Viv were still arguing poison versus possession when they were interrupted.

"Soak in an oatmeal bath for twenty minutes."

"Nana!"

"I'm home, Sweetie Boy. Give me a hug."

"How did you get here?" was all Lance was able to ask.

"This nice young man gave me a ride." George nodded from the doorway. "I still have my key."

Vivica froze when she saw the Easter. The sound of a rattle echoed in her brain. Phanny wanted to run for it. Margaret got the vapors.

"Don't worry, Mrs. Lakeland," George told Viv. "We know you don't practice law anymore. We were going to send you a note. Just get yourself some clothes and a name and go on about your life."

Vivica's knees buckled. Lance caught her and lowered her to the floor.

"Don't worry, Dear, I have exactly what you need." Lance's grandmother retrieved a tan- and-white puppy from under George's arm and put it in Viv's lap. "His name is Rusty."

George left them to their family reunion. He had a bus filled with family reunions waiting at the curb.

George had worried about the dogs and cats he had "rescued" and concocted elaborate tales of distant relocations and arduous journeys that precluded the oldsters from reclaiming their former pets. He was surprised by the ease with which they accepted his transparent fabrications.

Their first stop, after leaving Golden Slope, had been the Humane Society, where any senior who wished, picked out a pet. As they re-boarded the bus with arms full of soft fur or silken hair, Pom-Pom's mistress gently pulled George aside. "Do you mind if we have a few minutes alone on the bus? We'd like to say good-bye to each other."

"Of course. I'm sorry. I should have thought..."

"Five minutes, George, that's all we need."

While George watched animal technicians play with abandoned kittens, his friends on the bus swore a solemn oath.

"So it's agreed? We'll never tell him we know?"

"Of course not. We love him."

"Even though he lied?"

"Even though."

CHAPTER 23

RESTLESS

Milton turned off his tape recorder. He did not want this conversation in his memoirs. "The little freak could have killed himself, Schweppy. That's not supposed to happen. No one is supposed to die."

Irwin removed his glasses and massaged the indentations on the bridge of his nose with a thumb and forefinger. Bambi once tried to convince him contact lenses were more fashionable, but he didn't care. He had tried a pair twenty years earlier for an hour, and they hurt. "It would have been an accident, Milty. No one could fault us for that."

"I couldn't live with it. It was my Marge that let him wear that thing on his head. She would never have forgiven herself."

"Milt's right." Leon looked up from his computer terminal. "You can't kill off the world's most beloved superstar and expect people to like you. We've got to be more careful."

"Yeah," Milt said. "The little sneak kind of grows on you after a while. Reminds me of a puppet I had as a kid. He doesn't know how to behave with no one to pull his strings. And that sweet Chelsea Dove—Marge says she's starving herself."

A commotion and the slam of a door drew the attention of the men to the back of the auditorium where two women were dragging a struggling man toward the stage. At first glance, Milt thought the man was wearing a black *yarmulke*. As they moved closer, Milt could see that it was not a Jewish beanie, but what appeared to be a tight-fitting skullcap. Irwin put his glasses on for a better view. When the frenetic little group was within earshot of the stage, Marguerite held the prisoner around the neck while the sweet Chelsea Dove spoke.

"You'd better do something about this little fucker, or we're going to cut off his balls and slice them into the Jell-O salad."

Milton leaped from the stage to save Ricky Johnson from strangulation once again. Irwin took off his glasses again and wiped them with his shirttail. Either dirty specs impaired his vision, or the strange little entertainer had painted his head black from his forehead back to the nape of his neck.

"All right, all right." Milt easily peeled Marguerite's fleshy arm from around Ricky's throat. "You okay, Ricky?"

Ricky coughed. "Call me Rick."

Guilt washed over Milton like the wake of the Queen Mary. Obviously, the turban tourniquet had damaged the superstar's voice. "Here, sit down." He pulled down a plush seat in the front row. "Can I get you a lozenge?"

"He doesn't need a lozenge. He needs a hooker," said Chelsea.

"He needs a veterinarian. To neuter him," Marguerite added.

"What's wrong with his head?" Leon asked.

"Quiet!" Irwin yelled over the confusion. He sat down at the edge of the stage, feet dangling. He studied the exotic specimen in front of him through clean spectacles. There had been rumors, always denied, that the singer used exotic and dangerous creams to lighten his skin. Rick looked up at Irwin, his face a shining moon of desperation against the darkness of his scalp, a negative Al Jolson begging Sonny Boy to "climb upon my knee."

⌘⌘⌘

MOONLIGHT BOWL MANIFESTO

The barber had done her best to save Rick's hair, but the damage was too extensive and her awe of the Superstar too overwhelming.

Rick kept his eyes tightly closed as she ran the clipper, buzzing and tickling across his scalp. Later, she would sweep the fallen hair into a plastic bag for resale to his adoring fans. As she cut her first swath, she gaped at what was revealed beneath the thick layer of thatch—his true skin color. She saw in the mirror that his eyes were still closed and she continued. When the clipper had done its best, she applied shaving cream to the remaining stubble, using slow, swirling motions with a soft brush.

Rick relaxed and enjoyed the experience. His whole body hummed from the ministrations to his head. When the comely young woman used a silky whisk to remove stray hairs from his scalp and neck, he imagined her breasts whispering against her satiny smock. As he had never imagined a breast before in his entire life, Rick was confused. He had seen plenty of boobs in his Las Vegas show, but until now had only thought of them as convenient places to hang pasties. He fidgeted in his chair when she massaged cool, slippery oil into his newly-exposed pate. He visualized, and could almost feel, her strong fingers trailing gently down from his neck, to his chest, unbuttoning his shirt. He tugged at the crotch of his jeans, suddenly needing to make more room in the area of his lap, and he finally began to understand the words to some of his songs.

"You need a shave." His vision smacked him on the top of his head with her open palm. She had watched his expression change from trepidation to revelation and get a little too close to exaltation.

The slap jolted Rick's eyes open. A startled man looked

back at him from the mirror. He slid his hand over his glistening scalp and stared at it, expecting to see black rubbed off on his fingers.

The barber stepped back and studied Rick's bald head. "Maybe it'll fade after it's been exposed to sunlight for a while."

"I don't think so," Rick said.

"Well, your hair will grow back. Maybe you'll be allowed to wear some kind of a hat until then."

"I don't think so," said Rick again, remembering the turban incident.

"Anyway, as long as you're here, let me get those chin whiskers for you."

⌘⌘⌘

"Tell me what happened. Calmly," Irwin asked Chelsea.

"We went out of our way this morning to help this ungrateful little shit." Chelsea explained what had happened after they found Ricky in the laundry room. "After we dropped him off for his haircut, we decided to run track." The groundees were allowed access to all of the exercise and sporting facilities at the Center. When Irwin looked surprised, she added. "I run, Marguerite counts laps."

"I'm sorry," Ricky chimed in before his crime was revealed, hoping fervently that the apology lesson Milton taught him covered this kind of circumstance.

"Shut up, Ricky." Irwin said.

"It's Rick."

"Shut up, Rick. Go ahead, Miss Dove."

"Afterward, we took a shower."

"Both of you?" Irwin asked.

116

MOONLIGHT BOWL MANIFESTO

"Watching people run makes Marguerite sweat. Anyway, we catch this bowling-ball-head peeking at us through a slit in a locker."

"Ricky Johnson? Are you sure?"

"It's Rick."

"Shut up, Rick," chorused everyone in the room.

"Either you take care of him," Chelsea ordered, "or we will. Remember, there's always room in Jell-O."

Irwin, Milton, Leon and Ricky all crossed their legs.

The men waited until the women left the auditorium. Milton pulled the woeful miscreant to his feet and marched him up the steps to center stage where Irwin and Leon joined them.

"Ricky...Rick Johnson, raise your right hand over your head," Irwin commanded. Rick raised a trembling arm, worried about what else might be cut off today.

"All right Rick!" Irwin high-fived the outstretched hand.

"Today you are a man!" Leon added his five.

"But if you ever spy on Chelsea Dove, or anyone else again," Milton slapped a little bit harder than necessary for male camaraderie, "I'll hand you over to the women and spoon-feed you the Jell-O when they're finished."

"You're all pigs." The whooping celebrants had not heard Bambi come in. She was dressed in anonymous denim and polyester.

CHAPTER 24

THE EXPERIMENT

Irwin had a theory that Jesus Christ was an alien visitor from a planet with a really bizarre sense of humor. Earth was the playing field for a game of cosmic Monopoly, and Jesus had been sent to help write the rulebook.

⌘⌘⌘

"In Santa Clara today, an alert neighbor saved a four-year-old child from drowning." The President watched the satellite feed from a comfortable chair in the Oval Office.

"Young Agnes Glass wandered away from her nanny this morning and fell into the family pool while reaching for a floating toy. A neighbor two houses down, Bertha Waves, heard the splash while she was sunbathing in her backyard."

The President turned to the FBI agent. "Agnes? Bertha?"

"Yes, Sir," the agent answered. "Their new Nate names. Formerly Tiffany and Amber."

The newscast continued with an interview of a woman in a thong bikini. *"So I hear the splash, and I go 'What's that?' And I look up and see this kid and I go '(Bleep), she's drownin'.' So I run over to the pool and she goes 'Help,' so I go 'I'll save you.' And I do."*

The news anchor smiled into the lens. *"Our Hero of the Week, Bertha Waves. As an interesting sidebar to this story, it seems that the nanny, an illegal Indonesian immigrant, had been sold to the Glass family for fifteen hundred dollars. The*

Glasses warned her that if she went outside, she would be arrested and tortured by the police and deported. Immigration authorities are investigating."

The President turned down the volume. "We interviewed her?"

"Yes, Sir." The agent consulted his notes. "She said pretty much the same as the others. If the fence had been up, she'd have ignored the splash."

"And the lawyers?"

"Yep, she mentioned them. With the lawyers gone, she wasn't afraid of getting sued for trying to help."

"So, what do you think? Is this Schwep guy nuts? Or is he on to something here?"

"I can't say, Sir, but the numbers are pretty impressive."

"Tell me."

"Burglaries are down forty percent in California."

"How?"

"Well, before the fences came down, a burglar could duck into a backyard, take his time breaking into a house, snatch a VCR or some jewelry, make himself lunch and have a swim before he left."

"What about neighbors? Or alarms?"

"You don't make friends with neighbors you can't see, Sir. We're talking about eight-feet high privacy fences here. And the alarms? It's easier to ignore something you hear than something you can see. If you see a man beating his wife, you'll probably react, call the police, and get involved. If you *hear* a man beating his wife, you convince yourself it's not what you think, it's none of your business. If you hear a splash, it's an avocado or orange dropping from a tree. If you see a child drowning, you help."

"More numbers. Give me more numbers."

"School attendance is up thirty percent. Gang violence, down fifty percent."

"Are you serious?" The President leaned forward in his chair. "What have fences to do with schools or gangs?"

"It's the clothes, Sir. All the kids are dressed alike, now. The poorer children aren't ashamed to go to school. They're all in the same boat. You can't make fun of someone who looks exactly like you."

"You can't tell me that the Easters got the gang bangers to conform. They wouldn't care if Schwep blew up the whole state and killed every hostage, as long as their turf was left alone."

"Exactly, Sir. However, since no one in California is wearing logo jackets and million-dollar tennis shoes anymore, the bangers don't have anyone to maim and rob except each other.

"And that accounts for a fifty-percent drop in violent crime?"

"That, and the fact that they lost one of their deadliest weapons."

"What's that?"

"The lawyers."

⌘⌘⌘

The lawyers were being held in one of those big square states, east enough of California to be called 'back East,' and west enough of Chicago to be called 'out West'—but, their exact location was a closely guarded secret. With a population of well over one hundred thousand demagogues, pettifogs and those who only went to law school because they couldn't figure out computers, the encampment was larger than most towns and many cities. The detainees were orderly, if noisy. The indigenous animals had fled to the surrounding hills upon arrival of the cacophonous caravans. The incessant hissing of "sue, sue, sue" prompted the local rattlesnake population to abdicate to a worthier king.

As the purpose of their isolation was rehabilitation, not punishment, the men and women of the Bar were encouraged to participate in evening recreation; their mornings were spent in calisthenics, their afternoons at attitude adjustment seminars. During the first night's hootenanny, the retro-folk singer began his set with a Beatles' song:

> *Now somewhere in the Black Mountain hills of Dakota*
> *There lived a young boy named Rocky Raccoon.*
> *And one day his woman ran off with another guy;*
> *Hit young Rocky in the eye: Rocky didn't like that.*
> *He said, "I'm going to get that boy."*

The trouble started with a sniggering remark from the back of the audience. "If Rocky were my client, we'd sue for ten million."

"If Rocky were your client," a disembodied voice challenged, "he'd need ten million to keep himself out of jail."

"If he was my client, he'd take the fifth," said a gentleman noted for defending the 'connected,' believing they were discussing somebody named Rocko.

The singer turned up the speaker volume. His acoustical guitar competed with prosecuting attorneys yelling "aggravated assault," defense lawyers screaming "reasonable response," and civil libertarians whining "racism." By the time

MOONLIGHT BOWL MANIFESTO

Rocky found Gideon's Bible, the constitutionalists and rigid constructionists had added Separation of Church and State to the uproar. Divorce attorneys argued alienation of affection and questioned whether common-law marriages were recognized in the Black Mountain hills of Dakota. Curled fists cross-examined smug faces as egos clashed and junior partners failed to yield to seniors. Noses bled and ribs cracked when pinstriped civility and loop-holed frustration gave way to primal pummeling. Kings of the court grappled in the dust with worthy adversaries and honorable gentlemen; esteemed women counselors kicked at the crotches of distinguished jurists.

From the surrounding hills, the rattlesnakes watched in admiration.

The day following the melee found the combatants bandaged, swollen and more than a little ashamed. Morning exercise had mercifully been limited to a slow march along an abandoned mining trail; the procession was quiet, almost reverent. The marchers were given colorful bandannas to sop the sweat from their necks and twist the dust from clogged nostrils. The bright cloths hung limp from blue-jeans pockets and trailed from waistbands like flags of defeated nations. There was no more talk of litigation. Each penitent kept his own counsel. One Easter escort commented to another, "Let he who is without sin..."

After a purifying soak in an icy mountain stream and a chuckwagon lunch of franks and beans, the lawyers were ready for their first attitude adjustment seminar. Most of the participants attended seminars regularly even before the revolution and had run across burning coals and with wolves, scaled mountains, ingested mind-altering drugs, baked in mud, sweated in huts and held back urine in the quest for self-empowerment. The Easters had no such plans for spiritual enlightenment. They were hoping for common sense.

The lecturer surveyed the battered, chagrined crowd in front of him. His timing could not have been better. He pointed to the seminar title chalked on a giant blackboard:

These Things Happen.

⌘⌘⌘

Calls to the Frankly Fat talent agency had increased tenfold since the revolution began. Projects featuring the stars being held at the Center were put in abeyance until "this thing with the Easters" could be worked out. Until a compromise was reached, studio moguls, who were now controlled by Easters, mandated the hiring of *zaftig* actors for leading roles. Frankly Fat had been handling large-sized performers and models for many years, but until now had been limited to securing parts for good-natured sidekicks, or chubby next-door neighbors. Many of its clients had been forced to take modeling jobs for humorous greeting card companies or as gag strippers. Now studios were begging, "I need a two-hundred-pound Juliet," or "Send me a new James Bond with love handles and a gut," or "What I really need is a Marguerite type."

⌘⌘⌘

"Yesterday, two El Segundo men who were separated at birth thirty years ago, were reunited. The twins, born in the days before an 'unwed mother' became a 'single mom' were given up for adoption. The brothers discovered each other accidentally while mowing their lawns. Yes, that's right. They had been living backyard to backyard for the last five years, but,

until the fences came down, were unaware of each other's existence.

"And finally, a spokesman for the California Restaurant Association today announced a forty-two percent rise in business since the Easter takeover. Remember viewers, the next time you suggest 'Let's do lunch,' an Easter escort will be there to make sure you do."

The newscaster smiled like a best friend. *"...and now, for the national news."*

The President clicked off the set.

BARBARA JONES

CHAPTER 25

RUNNING

Chelsea pulled on clean socks and pushed her feet into a pair of communal sneakers. The shoes were sprayed between users, but Chelsea was still grateful for the barrier provided by the soft, absorbent cotton socks. After her run, the shoes would be returned to the bin marked size six, and the socks deposited in a hamper for laundering. She was allowed to run for only an hour a day, but she had learned that when the Easters changed shifts she could sneak another hour without detection. Her body had become so emaciated that a keen observer could see her heart beat through her shirt as she ran. She bent to tie the frayed laces and felt the swirling heaviness in her head that usually signaled a blackout; euphoria engulfed her and a million pinpoints of light skittered behind her closed eyelids. There was not enough liquid left in her starving frame to make sweat. Her skin was dry and cold.

"Hey, Slats, you look like Death." Marguerite stood over Chelsea with a glass of water and a wet cloth. "Hey, come on now. No kidding. Drink this."

Chelsea felt a sudden coolness as Marguerite stepped between her and the sun. A voice echoed around her but did not connect to her consciousness. A damp towel bathed her face.

"You're freaking me, Bones." Marguerite supported Chelsea's chin with her hand and poured water into her mouth. Reflexively, Chelsea began to sip and then to gulp. "That's it. Suck it up."

Chelsea gagged when Marguerite tipped the glass for maximum flow. "You're choking me, you cow."

"That's the old Chelsea the tabloids love. Haven't you

heard? Fat is in. Do yourself a favor, eat a grape. Knock yourself out; eat two, Brute."

Chelsea crossed her foot on her knee and finished tying her shoelace.

"Come on, Chels, you're not making any sense; shit, you're not even making nonsense. You won't make it halfway round the track."

Chelsea tied the other lace.

"Okay, kill yourself. We'll just sharpen your head to a point and pound you into the ground."

Chelsea felt the blood course through her body as she ran; it pulsed at her throat and rushed behind her ears. Through translucent skin she watched it race along the throbbing veins of her wrists. Her lungs burned and her stomach contracted into a hard knot indifferent to food. Her brain had shut off the desire for outside nourishment; her body was eating itself. Fat reserves depleted, her body now digested muscle. Skin rested painfully on bones and nerves. The heavy seams of her denim jeans bruised her hips and thighs. Yet still she ran—away from her needy, clinging mother; from her demanding agent; from screaming fans wanting to touch her; from the press; from big people with big shadows. But the faster she ran, the sooner she arrived back at the beginning.

Marguerite adjusted the rubber belt hidden under her shirt as she leaned back to watch Chelsea run. She was surprised to discover she could fit a hand between the rubber spikes and her body and slide the weight-loss device easily around her circumference. She hadn't been officially dieting since the cafeteria ladies had refused to divide her meals into fifty tiny medicine cups and ration her one cup every two minutes as decreed by the Beg For It diet. Her attempt at the All-You-Can-Eat-In-Thirty-Seconds diet had resulted in an unchewed potato being Heimliched into a chandelier. While the food at the Center was nourishing, it was limited to three meals a day and no alcohol. The kitchens were guarded, and Marguerite's midnight claims of tapeworm-induced starvation were ignored. As she watched Chelsea compulsively orbit the infield like a planet magnetically compelled to circle until allowed to crash into the sun, Marguerite kneaded the folds of her flesh and wondered what they were serving for dinner.

⌘⌘⌘

Lance and Vivica (now called Betty) tried to explain to Velma/Veronica why the missing Mr. Lakeland's picture could not be put on a milk carton.

"Because he's a pig, Mother," Betty/Vivica explained.

"*Because he's a food product,*" Phanny added *sotto voce.*

"That's only his terrestrial manifestation," Velma/Veronica said.

Lance flicked a dollop of dried oatmeal from his forearm. The soothing baths Nana Cornell had recommended for his rash were working so well he was developing a plan to re-package the cheap cereal and market it as an all natural organic miracle treatment. Not only was the itching gone, his skin had never been softer. He was still waiting for a return call from the Frankly Fat Agency regarding a spokesperson for his product.

"Don't forget about the insurance company, Velma," Lance appealed to her convoluted logic. "You don't want them to know your husband is still alive."

"But, technically, didn't they pay me for his dead body? It's his soul that possesses the pig."

"And possession is nine tenths of the law," Betty/Vivica quipped.

"What the hell does that mean? Velma/Veronica asked.

"I have no idea, Mother. Do you really want to argue metaphysics with an insurance adjuster?"

"What happens if you don't pay the exorcist?" Phanny asked Betty/Vivica's subconscious, and then answered her own question. *"You get repossessed."*

Betty/Vivica chuckled at the feeble joke only she and Margaret Mitchell could hear.

"What's so funny?" Velma/Veronica asked.

"Life, Mother. Life."

Nana Cornell listened to the discussion from behind a cracked bedroom door. "Do you believe these people, Rusty?" she whispered into her puppy's ear. "And they put *me* in a home."

⌘⌘⌘

Ethel/Serene was too excited to play her vitamin game with Goty and instead threw the tablets into the flushing toilet and giggled as the befuddled bulldog tried to lap them from the swirling waters. "Come on, Goty. The men are here to fix the yard so you can go out without your leash."

Ethel watched the men bury a cable around the perimeter of the small lot and then stick flags in the ground every few feet. By the time they were finished, Horace/Harmony was awake, fed, pharmaceutically reinforced and ready for a demonstration of the Park-A-Pet Containment System.

"You have to check the batteries periodically," the Park-A-Pet rep told him as he fastened the electronic collar around Goty's neck. "I've set the power level for the weight of your dog. When he nears the buried wire, a buzzer will warn him he's getting too close. If he tries to cross the line, he'll get a mild electric shock. The flags will help him learn his boundaries. After a week or so, the flags come down and your dog is trained to stay where he belongs. Please remember, we take no responsibility if these collars are used incorrectly. They are not to be used on children."

Goty shook his head at the unaccustomed weight of the electronic device, but was soon distracted by a chattering squirrel taunting him from a neighboring yard. As he raced toward his prey he heard an annoying buzzing sound and felt searing pain as his barrel-shaped body shot straight up into the air for ten feet then dropped to the ground where it lay convulsing, wisps of smoke curling from singed paws.

"Don't worry," the Park-A-Pet man said. "Sometimes we need to readjust the voltage level."

⌘⌘⌘

George and the guys had respectfully named them Council of the Elders, but they good-naturedly called themselves Coot Court. The youngest was seventy-five years old and the oldest couldn't remember his age but had flashbacks of San Juan Hill. However, he wasn't sure if he had actually been there or had played the part of Teddy Roosevelt in *Arsenic and Old Lace*. The Council was created to settle the petty bickering that was becoming endemic among the groundees. The twelve members were former retirement home residents with combined life experiences of almost one thousand years.

"So tell me, Mr. Johnson, why are you here today? Please forgive us if we finish our lunch while you answer. We've been very busy." The chairman put a spoonful of Jell-O into his mouth and sucked it back and forth through his teeth. His eleven associates followed suit. Irwin had briefed them about Chelsea's threat to turn Ricky's testicles into a salad ingredient.

Ricky, betrayed by his testosterone, looked up at the oldest people he had ever seen. They were seated at a long table on a dais stage left. Ricky stood under a spotlight at center stage. He had tried his best to control his behavior after the incident in the women's locker room, but his hormones had other plans. The appendage he had heretofore used only for bladder relief had become a divining rod that rose of its own volition and pointed in the direction of trouble. He was caught in the shower room again, huddled in a corner, disguised as a pile of dirty towels. He might have gotten away with it, if last year's Miss Universe hadn't chosen that moment to demonstrate to a former Miss World the proper way to do a breast exam.

"There's been some sort of a misunderstanding," Rick lied. "I was checking for mildew on the damp floor."

"Tie a knot in it, you little weasel," Miss World yelled from the fifth row. "That wasn't mildew on the floor."

"Order!" The chairman was enjoying his new position as mediator. Three weeks earlier, his biggest decision had been whether to nap with teeth in or teeth out. "Mr. Johnson, what are we to do with you?" The chairman tapped the side of his bowl of Jell-O with his spoon.

Rick hung his head and shrugged his shoulders. The elders pushed or wheeled their chairs into a tight circle to consider his case. After several minutes of whispered conversation and reminiscences of their own youthful peccadilloes, the council reached a decision.

"Ricky Johnson, straighten those shoulders." Rick pulled himself to attention. "Ricky Johnson, you're going to camp."

"It's Rick," the defendant whispered.

CHAPTER 26

CAMP

The arrival of the Nates and their escorts was the biggest thing to hit West Moon, Arkansas, since it beat out Moon as the site of the new Wal-Mart. West Moon had split from Moon seventy years earlier, when Cletis Moon decided to marry an outsider, a girl from Baxter County. The two towns had been rivals ever since.

West Moon was considered the more cosmopolitan, possessing, besides the Wal-Mart, a Wendy's, Burger King, Shoney's and McDonald's. West Moondians had even been known to marry folk from as far away as east Tennessee and south Louisiana. One man, returning from a stint in the Marine Corps, brought home a bride from Albany, Georgia. In contrast, the gene pool in Moon was so shallow, it was more of a gene slick than a gene pool. At large family gatherings, Moon children had to wear name tags to identify them to their own parents, although Eddie Pearl Moon swore she could identify her own by smell. On the upside, however, family photos were interchangeable.

The bus station was located by mutual agreement in West Moon, since no one in Moon ever went farther than the county seat, and then usually in the back of a squad car to jail on drunk and disorderly charges, and they were fetched home by irate wives in Bondoed Chevies or rusted-out pickup trucks.

No Moon man had served in the military since the Civil War. Inbreeding had given them all a genetic predisposition for flat feet and deafness in one ear. However, they all considered themselves patriotic, God-fearing Americans.

The bus station had a small waiting room, and a bathroom scrupulously cleaned by the Ladies Auxiliary of the West Moon Hunting, Fishing and Tourism Council. Bus tickets had to be purchased at the drugstore across the street. Today, the mayor, and three men and two women from the Tourism Council, waited patiently for the bus. The men discussed the benefits of the visit on the future of West Moon. The women prayed quietly that the Moons would stay on their side of the river.

⌘⌘⌘

The Grand Buck of the BBB flicked his lighter and held it an inch away from the creature's head. Disoriented by the flame, the scorpion arched its segmented tail inward and stung itself to death.

"Godammit, Arliss, I asked you not to torture critters in my shop." The proprietor of the One-O-One Gun and Pawn swept the dead arachnid onto a piece of cardboard and flung it out the door.

"You get yourself a cat, you won't be gettin' no more stingers in here." Arliss pushed the wad of tobacco he kept in his mouth to his left cheek with his tongue, and spat a cancerous stream of foul-smelling, coffee-colored juice into the thirty-two ounce Coca-Cola cup he held in his hand.

"I get myself a cat, your Junior'll be shavin' it and hanging it in a tree 'fore it's old enough to hunt."

"Yeah, that kid, he's sumpin'." Arliss wiped dark brown spittle from the crease at the corner of his mouth. "I come for my gun."

"It's twenty dollars, same as always." The broker pulled a pawn receipt from the file he kept under the counter.

MOONLIGHT BOWL MANIFESTO

"I ain't paying interest today. I'm pickin' up."

The broker was worried. His customers usually pawned their deer rifles the day after gun season ended and paid interest on them each month until the next year's season, even though the accrued monthly interest often exceeded the amount of the loan, and sometimes the value of the gun. They only picked them up between seasons if they were leaving town or looking for trouble. Arliss was a Moon, so that only left trouble.

⌘⌘⌘

Lance and Betty/Vivica read bumper stickers to amuse themselves as they crossed the country in a chartered bus. While they were still in California, the stickers pleaded with them to "Save the Whales," "Protect the Ozone" and "Think Green." The farther east and south they traveled, the more Biblical and violent the messages became. In Arizona they proclaimed, "Jesus Loves You" and "Nuke Jane Fonda." Apparently, Jesus didn't love Jane Fonda.

"I don't think we're in Kansas anymore, Toto," Betty/Vivica told Lance when she spotted a sticker that read "Dead Faggot in Trunk" somewhere in Texas. "I think we'd better pretend we're a couple from now on."

"Don't be ridiculous, Viv. This is the new millennium."

"Well, at least change your shirt."

An underground market was burgeoning on the West Coast for counterfeit bowling shirts of one hundred percent cotton or pure silk. An old lover of Lance's from San Francisco had sent him one with the name of a fictitious styling salon, The Blow and Go, emblazoned across the back. Lance now alternated wearing the comfortable cotton shirt with a polyester one issued by the Easters.

When the bus reached Oklahoma City, Betty/Vivica jabbed Lance sharply in the ribs and pointed at the message riding the bumper of a grimy van in front of them: "God Created Each Man for a Purpose: Queers Make Great Fertilizer."

"Wanna go steady?" Lance asked her as he reached for his spare shirt.

Velma/Veronica endured the journey with varying degrees of comfort and consciousness. Her pants legs were lined with cellophane packets of pills taped to the denim, making it difficult to bend her knees. She explained her extra bulk— and her frequent, stiff-legged trips to the bathroom— by claiming water retention. After each visit to the restroom, she returned to her seat either happier or drowsier.

Phanny didn't care where they were going; she was enjoying the ride. The bus reminded her of the sixties and her flower-painted Volkswagen van. On this trip, however, when she flashed the peace symbol to the car next to them, a man in his undershirt waved a shotgun back at her. Margaret Mitchell was hoping their destination was Atlanta, Georgia, or Charlottesville, Virginia. Her first choice would be Virginia. She had read on a book jacket that it was the home of Alexandra Ripley. Phanny had convinced her that if she confronted Ms. Ripley in person and demanded a public apology for *Scarlett*, then maybe her spirit could rest and she could return to the astral plane whence she came. If they didn't reach Charlottesville, Atlanta would be all right, too. Margaret heard that some Germans had rebuilt the arson-destroyed apartment building she had lived in while writing *Gone with the Wind*. She'd have to remember her matches.

Ricky Johnson (or 'Just Rick,' as he had introduced himself to Vivica/Betty, Velma/Veronica and Lance) was traveling incognito. His former, familiar soprano voice had become a consistent baritone. A short growth of black curls covered the bizarre darkness of his scalp. Sideburns, and a nicely developing beard and mustache, helped disguise the delicate features of his face. Milton sat in the aisle seat next to Rick, hemming him in. Milt wasn't afraid that he, or any of the Nates, would try to escape; too many escorts and too many groundees were still being held at the Center. Milton was afraid Rick would harass the female passengers. At one refueling and leg-stretching stop, a truck driver caught the hormone-inspired Johnson looking down the blouse of the big-haired girl working the register at Stuckey's. He swore he had dropped a mint down there. Only Milt's insistence that their group was on a field trip from a mental institution, and a fifty-dollar bill for the big-haired girl, saved Rick from becoming fossil fuel.

⌘⌘⌘

The BBB (Big Bad Bubbas) was founded by Arliss Moon's daddy because he thought the KKK was getting "way too lib'ral." Arliss inherited the title of Grand Buck when his daddy was killed in a freak still explosion that blew him into unrecognizable bits, although his wife was able to identify him later when they found a finger wearing his wedding ring perfectly preserved in a jar of moonshine. All of the BBB were Christians, which meant, on the Moon side of the river, that their wives went to church every Sunday, and the men knew enough Bible verses to support their ignorance. Not only did they hate anyone who wasn't white, Anglo-Saxon/American/Christian, they were suspicious of people with arches who could hear out of both ears. Arliss had called an emergency meeting of the BBB when he heard some of those "tree-huggin'

California commies" would be staying in West Moon for a while.

They met in an abandoned, decaying barn that folks used for illegal cock fights and Junior Moon used to shave his animals. Junior was obsessed with skin. There wasn't a cat, dog, sheep, pig or squirrel that was safe from his razor. Junior believed, after spending many hours in the bathroom with *The National Geographic,* that if he could get himself a monkey, he could prove that, under the hair, you'd find an African Pygmy. He was beaten soundly each time he voiced this blasphemous theory.

⌘⌘⌘

The bus pulled in as the Tourism Council was discussing whether to first take the visitors to feed the tame carp at Bull Shoals State Park or to Hillbilly Willy's to buy souvenir hats and keychains. Because Irwin had spoken with the mayor by telephone and requested that the campers be allowed to keep a low profile, Milton was surprised to see a welcoming committee and high-school marching band waiting for them at the station. He was not as surprised, however, as the sleeping passengers who were jolted awake by crashing cymbals and cheap musical instruments eviscerating John Philip Sousa. As the groggy travelers stumbled from the bus into the blazing Arkansas sunshine, adjusting underwear, stretching cramped necks and arms, and punching sleep-numbed thighs, they were each presented with a welcome gift. Each basket contained muffins, homemade walnut-peanut butter fudge, coupons for free dinners at Ray's House of Catfish, and twelve free minnows from the Bait Barn.

While the mayor gave his speech, Velma/Veronica and

MOONLIGHT BOWL MANIFESTO

Betty/Vivica mentally criticized the attire of the crowd; Rick eyed the baton twirlers; Milton surreptitiously nibbled pieces of muffin, and Lance stared in horror at two bald young men hovering on the fringe of the crowd. "Skinheads!" he whispered to Betty/Vivica, spearing her ribs with a bony elbow.

"Don't you fret, Darlin'." A member of the Ladies Auxiliary had overheard Lance's worried whisper and rushed to reassure him. "They're just Moon boys." She patted his hand. "They wear their hair like that to hold off the lice."

Phanny was repulsed. Margaret was delighted to finally hear someone speaking English with the correct accent.

BARBARA JONES

MOONLIGHT BOWL MANIFESTO

CHAPTER 27

COLD

Chelsea was not intimidated by the weather report. She'd been to Aspen. She had felt the invigorating rush of wind whipping past her as she streaked colorfully down a mountain in bright, designer skiwear. The cold air only made the hot rum drinks around the fire in the lodge more inviting. She leaned her cheek against the window of the airplane and watched the lights of O'Hare Airport get bigger and brighter as the airliner made its approach.

Even as a child, Marguerite hated the cold. She abhorred the little shaving nicks of pain as fingers thawed out; she detested the styptic pencil sting of warmth returning to frozen limbs. "Crisp," her grandparents called the numbing weather. "It has an edge to it." *So does a razor blade,* thought Marguerite as the plane taxied to the terminal, *but I wouldn't want that slicing through my body, either.*

As George pulled the heavy bags from the luggage carrousel, he wondered about the wisdom of Irwin's latest plan. After Ricky Johnson was sentenced to camp by Coot Court, Irwin decided that it would be a good idea to send all the Nates to experience how the real world lived.

While it sounded good in theory (and Irwin's theories always *sounded* good), George worried. The plan had to be modified when Leon reported that, although contributions were still pouring in, funds would not permit educating everyone. A lottery was held and Nates were dispersed to the hinterlands, as money would allow.

George snapped out of his reverie when a traveling

salesman fought him for the last suitcase catapulted onto the conveyor belt from Luggage Hell. George won possession by pointing out the yellow smiley-face sticker that Marge had applied to the bag for easy identification.

Flanked by Easter escorts, Horace/Harmony, Ethel/Serene, Chelsea and Marguerite watched the snow through the glass doors of the terminal as they waited for George. Still dressed in issued clothes, they shivered in their thin bowling shirts every time the automatic doors opened. They were ignored by crowds that rushed to grab cabs, meet friends, or were simply moving fast because fast is how you moved in Chicago.

George's pulse quickened as he negotiated the throng. He felt his body return to the old, frenetic rhythms of the city he loved. He brought his rented luggage cart to a halt in front of the Nates and began opening suitcases and handing out winter clothes: army surplus sweatshirts and coats; and lumpy hand-knitted scarves, mittens and hats made by former retirement home residents. The effect was martial, yet homey. "Be sure you wear the sweatshirts," he warned the Nates. "Layering is everything."

"Here, let me fix this," Marguerite told Ethel/Serene as she hitched up the struggling child's over-sized coat and secured it with her scarf.

"But, you'll need your scarf, Marguerite. You'll freeze." Ethel/Serene was both fascinated and horrified at the thought of temperatures lower than a refrigerator's.

"Nah, I was born in the Midwest. I can take it."

"Getting soft in your old age?" Chelsea asked as she watched Marguerite tuck the little girl's hair under her knit cap.

"At least I'll have an old age. You won't make it

through the winter." Marguerite clipped Ethel/Serene's mittens to her coat sleeve. "Someone's got to help. This kid's old man is useless."

"I teach my daughter to be independent. If there's a problem, she'll become one with the problem to get through the problem," Horace/Harmony said.

"I think you're the problem, Hor-ass," Marguerite emphasized the last syllable of his name.

Horace/Harmony flinched and silently cursed his great grandfather. "So, how come you didn't have to change your names?" he asked Chelsea and Marguerite.

"Because we're hostages, you schmuck. Isn't that punishment enough?"

"And how come you're even on this trip? You just said you were born in the Midwest. You're no Nate. You're an Easter."

"I'm a Nat."

"What the hell's that?"

"A naturalized Nate. Irwin says I've been in California long enough to adopt a screwed value system."

"That's skewed," George interrupted.

"Skew you," Marguerite retorted.

"All right, never mind. Our ride is here. Help me reload the cart." George turned in time to see a young boy pushing their cart away at breakneck speed and leaping on the back for a ride. He smiled. He had forgotten about the kids who worked the airport, asking for spare change and returning abandoned luggage carts for the fifty-cent deposit. Usually, though, they waited until passengers were through with them.

"All right, never mind. Help me carry these bags." George picked up a suitcase and led the way through the automatic doors, past the taxi and limo lines to a waiting hotel shuttle bus.

"Well, well." Marguerite nudged Chelsea and pointed to the logo of a luxury hotel painted on the side of the bus. "At least we'll be housed in style."

"Welcome to the Drake," the doorman greeted them an hour later as the shuttle driver piled their bags on the curb in front of the posh Michigan Avenue hotel.

"Hot damn! Chels," Marguerite said brightly. "I hope the masseuse is still on duty."

"Where's the exercise room?" Chelsea asked the doorman.

"Sorry, we won't be staying." George waved away an eager bellhop. "We've got another bus to catch," he told his stunned charges. "Grab a bag."

The pathetic little tribe huddled together under the bus route sign in front of the hotel, waiting for a northbound bus and praying for death. A previous snowfall had melted and refrozen, glazing the sidewalks. Chelsea and Ethel/Serene wrapped their arms around the signpost to keep the piercing Lake Michigan wind from skating them across the icy pavement into traffic. Horace/Harmony was sure his lungs had frozen when he inhaled the frigid air. He knew his nose would soon fall off and shatter into a million pieces on the ground. Marguerite could not uncurl her fingers inside her mittens, and Ethel/Serene had not felt her toes for at least ten minutes. Chelsea's tears of pain froze against her cheek. This was not Aspen.

"Step lively," George encouraged his group when the CTA bus finally arrived. "This isn't California. The driver won't wait for dawdlers." He needn't have worried. The Nates and escorts scrambled onto the bus faster than George could drop tokens into the fare box. Although the heater was broken, the crowded bus offered some protection against the fierce winds.

"That was close," George said later as the bus pulled away from their final stop of the day, Horace/Harmony's scarf trailing ominously from the closed exit doors. "I told you to step lively, didn't I?"

⌘⌘⌘

George smelled the pizza before he heard the delivery boy pound on the motel-room door.

"Yo! Pizza here."

"Come on in. Warm up for a minute." George took four steaming boxes from a young man wearing a Chicago Bulls baseball cap and put them on the radiator to keep hot, an old college trick.

The boy looked in at the figures draped in blankets and huddled around the radiator, warming their hands on the pizza boxes. *Tourists.* He winked at George. "What? Are you kiddin'? This is beach weather. Wait 'til it really gets cold."

After the boy collected his money and left, Horace/Harmony laid his cheek against a pizza box, and as the radiator hissed and gurgled, he sobbed quietly into his sleeve.

In the motel lobby, the delivery boy adjusted the battery pack on his heated vest, pulled up two pairs of heavy wool socks and chuckled at the gullibility of out-of-towners.

"Deli here!" Before George could pry the warm pizza boxes from the frozen Nates his order from the Thorndale Delicatessen arrived.

"What's wit' them?" A tiny, withered man wearing a Cubs jacket and earmuffs asked George as he handed over two large brown paper bags.

"Never mind them. Did you bring the pickles?"
"You order pickles?"
"Yes."
"Then you got pickles. They on drugs or somethin'?"
"They're just cold."
"With this heat wave?" The little man shrugged and left.

Marguerite helped George lay out their dinner across one of the two queen-sized beds. The opened pizza boxes put forth an aroma never smelled west of the state line. Large balls of fennel-laden Italian sausage nestled in a thick, spicy tomato sauce fought for space with generous slices of green peppers and mounds of fresh mushrooms and black olives. The toppings were piled so high on the thin crust that pieces of sausage were glued to the inside top of the box by melted cheese. Marguerite scraped a savory morsel free with her thumbnail and popped it into her mouth.

The ambrosial odor of secret pickling spices in the corned-beef sandwiches he was unwrapping evoked memories in George so strong he could actually see Abe standing behind the counter of his deli assuring his mother "Of course it's lean, would I sell you fatty?" He remembered staring at the faded numbers tattooed on the deli owner's forearm while his mom inquired about the freshness of the smoked chub. He remembered Abe shooing him and his friends out of the deli located across the street from Swift Elementary School after they had purchased a brownie with the dime their mothers had given them for a lunchtime treat.

"You go, get an education," Abe would order. If they hesitated, he flourished his meat cleaver at them. "Out! You should only miss the bell again, and the principal will be yelling on me not to let you in here." George and his friends would discuss later, at recess, if Abe had really once chopped off a kid's hand with the cleaver.

Horace/Harmony peeled back the top slice of rye bread from the thick, pungent sandwich Marguerite passed to him. "This paté is lumpy," he complained. "Anyway, do you know what they do to geese to get paté? They force feed them with a funnel."

"You're the goose, Hor-ass. That's chopped chicken liver, you lox." Marguerite took the sandwich from Horace and handed it to Chelsea. "Here, eat one of these, and you'll gain ten pounds."

Chelsea recoiled from the proffered delicacy and nibbled at a slice of green pepper picked from a pizza and meticulously wiped clean of calorie-laden cheese. She pulled tiny pieces of pepper skin free with her teeth and spent minutes grinding each minute portion into a digestible pulp she felt comfortable swallowing. She studied George as she chewed. She had noticed a difference in him since their arrival in Chicago. He walked and talked faster. It was subtle, but as an actress known for her facility with dialects, Chelsea could also hear changes in his accent. He was flattening his *A*'s by running them through his nasal passages. He was dropping the final *H* in *th* words, which allowed Bostonians, Chelsea supposed, free use of that letter to "pahk" their "cahs" in "Hahvahd Yahd."

Ethel/Serene stared at the mounds of exotic food. The round, heavenly-smelling objects in the boxes vaguely resembled the pizzas sold back home by a giant cartoon rat, but each of these Chicago pies held enough ingredients to make twelve rat pizzas. She bit off the point of the slice George handed her and watched helplessly as the toppings slid off the remaining portion onto the bedspread. "I'm sorry," she told George through a mouthful of pizza.

"You did that on purpose." Horace/Harmony grabbed the empty crust from his daughter and threw it in the brown-paper trash bag.

"Give the kid a break," Marguerite said and handed her another slice.

"No." Horace took the second slice and put it back in the box. "She's expressing her hostility toward me for leaving her mother. A fast will cleanse her aura." He reached for a corned-beef sandwich, took a bite and asked George, "Got any mayonnaise?"

"Excuse us," George said as he twisted his fist in the neck of Horace/Harmony's sweatshirt and pulled him to his feet. "Horace and I are going for a little walk."

Chelsea pulled her knees to her chest and spat masticated green pepper into a napkin. Marguerite silently handed Ethel/Serene another piece of pizza. The only sounds heard through the flimsy motel room door were the smack of a fist hitting flesh and an *A*-flattening voice yelling, "Mayonnaise! Wit' corned beef?"

The next morning, Horace/Harmony drew his hooded sweatshirt tightly over his swollen jaw and knelt to help Ethel/Serene tie up her coat. He wasn't sure if the previous night's right cross had been for his treatment of his daughter or his choice of condiments, so he wasn't taking any chances.

A tired band of Easters and Nates filed through the lobby doors to meet the mini-van for the continuation of their journey. Most of them had been up all night with heartburn. A brilliant winter sun bounced painfully off newly fallen snow, not yet trampled gray, and added headaches to their misery.

MOONLIGHT BOWL MANIFESTO

George issued sunglasses to his charges and handed each a bag containing coffee, bagels, a pint of orange juice and an Alka-Seltzer.

The van stopped in Green Bay, Wisconsin, for provisions around one o'clock that afternoon. For the rest of the trip, the passengers held large sacks of groceries on their laps and balanced others on the floor between their legs. It had started to snow in Sturgeon Bay, but still they headed north up the "thumb" of the state into Door County, past Ephraim, Egg Harbor, Little Sister and Sister Bay. The towns grew smaller and the snow fell heavier as they traveled. The van plowed slowly through thickening streets. Ethel/Serene watched out the window for polar bears and Eskimos. Marguerite used her knit cap to muffle the sound of crinkling cellophane as she filched cookies from the bag at her feet. Horace/Harmony slept and Chelsea counted her heartbeats as she tried to quiet the rushing in her ears. George worried that they wouldn't make Gills Rock before the last ferry run.

The ramp to the car-ferry glistened with salt as George backed the van carefully into the spot indicated by the captain. The van's passengers were already ensconced in the glass-enclosed cabin at the top of the boat. The only other vehicle on board was a Volvo belonging to the dentist who visited once a month to care for the islanders' teeth.

"Do you know why they called this place Door County?" the dentist asked his fellow passengers as the captain maneuvered the *Erybacki* away from the dock. "The Indians named this stretch of water Death's Door, because of all the ships that sunk here," he continued before anyone could answer.

Waning daylight and swirling snow soon made the *Erybacki* invisible from the dock. Sharp, loud cracking noises echoed from frozen shoreline cliffs as the massive ferry broke through five-foot deep ice. The sheared ice flashed blue and pink in the running lights, a miniature aurora borealis. Horace/Harmony traced the word "help" backwards on the frosty cabin window.

CHAPTER 28
SAVE YOUR CONFEDERATE MONEY THE SOUTH WILL RISE AGAIN

Junior Moon sat in a deer stand built ten feet from the ground in the branches of a scarred old oak. With him on the platform sat a cooler of Budweiser and a box of Kleenex. He drained a beer and threw the empty can at a hairless dog sleeping in the tangled roots at the base of the tree. The seventeen-year-old had switched to drinking beer after his granddaddy's moonshine vaporized his nose hairs and made him susceptible to colds. Wet tissues and crumpled cans littered the ground under the stand. He lit a cigarette and hung it from the corner of his mouth, away from his sensitive nostrils. He brought a pair of binoculars up to his eyes and continued his watch.

⌘⌘⌘

Lance and Betty/Vivica sat on a bench next to a statue of a confederate general. They were alone except for Margaret Mitchell and Phanny, who were quietly rehashing the Civil War in a tiny compartment of Betty/Vivica's brain.

"We could run away." Lance sucked strawberry soda through a straw and watched people squeezing fruit at the farmers' market set up on the town square.

"And go where? Home? They'd just pick us up again and send us someplace worse."

"Worse than here?" Lance shuddered, remembering the copperhead snake that had slithered across his path that morning, and the rustling sound the scorpion had made at the bottom of the paper grocery bag.

"It's not so bad here," Betty/Vivica said.

"Not so bad! I was almost killed. Twice."

"That snake wasn't going to bite you. They don't eat fruit. And by the time you finished jumping up and down on that bag, there was nothing left of that scorpion but smear. So much for your Greenpeace award," she sniffed. "You can be such a girl, sometimes."

"I was just about to reach into that bag, Viv. This close."

"Anyway, the groundskeeper at the lodge told you not to worry. He said they were harmless."

"I don't think 'Their venom prob'ly wouldn't kill an adult' is the same thing as harmless." Lance vacuumed the last of his drink from the bottom of the bottle and looked around for a recycling bin.

"Where'd you get that soda, anyway? We don't have any money."

"The guy in the gas station gave it to me when I went to pee. They're very friendly around here."

"Is he gay?"

"Who?"

"The gas station guy."

"Do you think gay people have some sort of built-in radar that goes off and tells them when someone is gay? Or maybe we have a secret code? Or handshake? Or maybe 'It takes one to know one?'"

"Well, maybe. After all, I can always spot someone who's had a boob job."

"Good point."

"So. Is he?"

"They have a very deep closet in this town, but if he isn't gay, he's at least mildly amused. But that's all neither here nor there. Weren't we talking about escape?"

"You were, Lance. Maybe you could hotwire a car."

"I don't know how."

"You sell cars for a living, for Christ's sake."

"Infinitis come with keys. And what would I do about gas?"

"Maybe your new boyfriend at the Texaco station could help."

"You're such a bitch sometimes, Viv."

"Don't worry, Sweetie. They'll send us home soon. Irwin promised."

"Margaret doesn't want to go home. She likes it here."

"Shut up, Phanny," Lance said. "Someone's coming."

A neat young woman wearing a Laura Ashley jumper over a while sailor blouse walked over to their bench. "Excuse me. Y'all are Nates, aren't you?"

"Yes, we all are Nates," Lance replied. "You all are very astute."

"Now, stop teasin' me. I can see by your armbands y'all are Nates. I just wanted to stop and invite you over to my house for lunch."

Out of my way! These are my people. I'm taking over, Margaret told Phanny and Betty/Vivica. *He doesn't even know that "y'all" is plural.*

"We'd be delighted to accept your kind invitation," Margaret answered aloud with her best southern manners.

"Yeah, sure. Anytime." Lance agreed, believing this to be the "Let's do lunch" game.

"Okay, then." The steel magnolia stood waiting. "My car's just acrossed the square."

"You mean today? Now?" Lance had been asked to

"do" lunch many times, but had never actually firmed up any invitations.

"Of course, Sugar. I wouldn't have asked you to dine if I didn't expect to see you sittin' at my table."

"I've got to find a recycling bin for my bottle, first."

"Just toss it in the trash, Honey. The only thing they recycle 'round here is the grease they cook the chicken in."

⌘⌘⌘

Junior Moon cupped a muscadine loosely in his left hand and squeezed a rock in his right. He bent his knees for better thrust and tossed the grape straight up into the air. Before he could hurl his rock, a tiny brown missile launched itself from its hanging place under the rotting rafters, trapped the grape in midair and continued its flight out of Junior's range. Junior's rock clattered harmlessly off the far wall, dispelling the rumor that he couldn't hit the broad side of a barn.

"I seen 'em, Daddy," he said, picking another grape from a bunch in the bucket at his feet. "He were talking to Eustis down to the Texaco station and she were talkin' in tongues all by her lonesome."

"Stop wasting them grapes, boy. You ain't never gonna get you no bat. They got radar. Makes 'em know when to duck." When Junior failed to respond, Arliss Moon walked around and spoke into his son's good ear, "Stop wasting good grapes on flying rats." Arliss cuffed Junior's good ear.

Junior shrugged, popped a purple fruit into his mouth, slipped the skin off with his tongue and spit the seeds on the floor. "What we gonna do, Daddy? There are sodomites in the land, giving themselves over to fornication, and going after strange flesh."

MOONLIGHT BOWL MANIFESTO

Arliss thwacked the boy on the side of his head again. "Don't you go quotin' Scriptures at me. I know what The Book says. What about her?"

"She's for sure a witch, Daddy. I seen her talking to spirits." Junior closed one nostril with a finger and blew snot from the other onto the floor.

"And when they shall say unto you, seek unto them that have familiar spirits, and unto wizards that peep, and that mutter..." Arliss quoted.

"Regard not them that have familiar spirits, neither seek after wizards, to be defiled by them." Junior shouted to the rafters, disturbing the sleeping bats. "Shit, Daddy," he yelped when his father smacked his ear for a third time. "Why'd you do that for? You know we only got one good ear apiece."

Arliss picked up a broken rake handle. "For every one that curseth his father or his mother shall be surely put to death." He brought the rod down hard on Junior's back. "He that spareth his rod hateth his son: but he that loveth him chasteneth him betimes."

"I love you, too, Daddy," Junior managed before he passed out.

BARBARA JONES

CHAPTER 29

ONWARD CHRISTIAN SOLDIERS

"'Bye! Are you sure I can't carry you over to the lodge? It looks like it's fixin' to storm. Oh, and don't mind about that Tupperware, drop it off anytime, or maybe I'll stop over and pick it up."

"No, no. We're fine. We'll walk. We need to work off that terrific lunch." Lance waved back at the woman and hissed to Betty/Vivica, "Walk faster, before she insists on driving us back."

"I can't walk any faster. I've just consumed enough fat grams to grease a GM plant. And whoever heard of a grown woman named Puddin'?"

"You didn't have to eat everything she put in front of you, and ask for seconds. And what about that house? It looked like Laura Ashley exploded in there."

"I never asked for seconds. They just appeared on my plate. Margaret Mitchell was the one doing all the eating. She must have asked for more."

"Can't you control your little friends?" Lance asked Betty/Vivica.

"I thought her home was charming," Margaret answered, "and the corn pudding was excellent."

"I was talking to Viv, you ignorant hillbilly," Lance said.

"Ignorant. Ha! Did you ever win a Pulitzer Prize?"

"Peace." Phanny held up two fingers in a *V*. "Can't we all just get along?"

As Phanny sang a John Lennon song about giving

peace a chance and Lance kicked a crumpled Red Man pouch along the road, a small group of hooded figures worked their way through the woods from the Moon side of the river.

⌘⌘⌘

Rick Johnson arched his back, clawed his hands and hissed at the cat that he was trying to imitate. When the cat ran into the woods, Rick jumped up on a stump, squatted and licked the back of his hands. He then leaped from the stump, spun around three times and curled himself into a ball on the ground.

Velma/Veronica applauded, splashing the drink she held in one hand. "Not bad, but I think I liked your chipmunk dance better."

The post-pubescent recording artist was choreographing new routines. He wanted to be ready when the Easters released them. "It would work better if I had a tail," he said, twisting his body to look at his backside.

"Keep drinking the water around here and you may grow one," Velma/Veronica said. "Have you noticed all the animals around here are bald? Stick with bourbon, I say." She toasted the air with her glass.

Rick, Velma/Veronica and Milton stuck close to the hunting lodge the city council had loaned them for their visit. Milton stayed busy dictating his memoirs into his tape recorder and writing love letters to Marge. Rick, afraid of being recognized, used his time to develop a new act to go with his new voice. Since running out of her pills, Velma/Veronica had discovered bourbon and spent most of her time trying to get out of a lawn chair. The Easter escorts played a great deal of poker.

"Help me out of this damn thing." Velma held out her drinkless hand to Rick. "It's time for *Days of Our Lives*."

MOONLIGHT BOWL MANIFESTO

After he pulled her free from the aluminum and mesh and led her to the door of the lodge, he noticed a rabbit moving along the road to town, stopping every few feet to nibble and sniff. *Yes,* he thought. *I could do that.* He followed the bunny, hopping, sniffing, hopping, sniffing.

⌘⌘⌘

"Jesus Christ, did we miss Halloween?" Lance put out his arm to stop Betty/Vivica and nodded toward the trees at the side of the road.

"Oh, Lord. It's them," Margaret answered for the trinity and dropped the leftover corn pudding she had been carrying.

"You're kidding, right? This is some kind of a fraternity prank? Chi Delta Klan?" Lance stared at the five costumed figures as they emerged from the thicket. One carried a deer rifle, three carried torches and ropes, the fifth clutched a box of Kleenex.

"Jesus Christ died for your sins," a muffled voice intoned ominously from under a pointed white hood.

"Yeah, well, he must have had a lousy lawyer," Lance joked. "This is some kind of a gag, right?"

Betty/Vivica screamed in terror and disbelief as the butt of a rifle opened the back of Lance's head.

"Then the Lord rained upon Sodom and upon Gomorrah brimstone and fire from the Lord out of heaven," the blood-spattered Grand Buck of the BBB pronounced over Lance's fallen body.

Betty/Vivica knelt and tried to stem the flow from her friend's wound. Her head snapped back sharply as a rope was thrown around her neck and pulled taut. She felt a foot in the middle of her back as the noose tightened. Something hard and

159

cold crunched her cheekbone. Then another rock hit her in the temple as she heard the muffled words: "A man also or woman that hath a familiar spirit, or that is a wizard, shall surely be put to death: they shall stone them with stones; their blood shall be upon them."

"It's okay, Viv, we're here," Phanny told her. "Margaret and I. We'll take care of you."

Then darkness.

⌘⌘⌘

Rick soon tired of following the rabbit along the rural highway. He decided that the woodland creatures of Arkansas were not masculine enough for his new image. He made up his mind to ask Irwin to send him to Africa to study the movements of big, ferocious, macho beasts. Maybe he could even find his roots, although with his white skin, he looked more like he had been grafted onto the family tree. A car passed, and Rick automatically raised his arm to wave back. When he first arrived in West Moon, he thought people waved at him in error, thinking they knew him; then he realized that it must be some kind of secret signal white people used with each other.

The afternoon sky had turned dark with an ominous tinge of green. Road litter swirled and danced as the wind picked up. When Rick finally looked up from the leathery carcass of an opossum he had been poking with a stick, he saw Betty/Vivica and Lance rounding a curve ahead of him, and was about to give them the Caucasian air-five when he spotted the BBB oozing from the woods. He dived into the ditch at the side of the road and crawled painfully through pine needles and cones until he reached the cover of the woods.

I don't really know those people all that well, he

thought as he worked his way through the pines back toward the lodge. *Milton will know what to do.* Then he heard Betty/Vivica scream, and a rush of pent-up testosterone pricked his conscience and girded his loins. There was no time for reinforcements. He'd have to save them himself. He stopped and turned back.

Rick shadowed the cloaked figures as they dragged two limp bodies away from the shoulder, through the woods into a clearing strewn with abandoned appliances and rusted out auto parts. He watched as the hooded figures lashed the Nates to rudely constructed crosses stuck into the soft loam of the forest floor and piled kindling around the crucifixes. When Betty/Vivica's head lolled to one side, Rick's hand flew to his throat as the rope burns around her neck evoked the memory of his own near-strangulation.

Enraged, he snatched up a corroded tail pipe and ran bellowing into their midst. "I am the god of hellfire!" he quoted from a rock-and-roll song of the sixties. However, his avenging sword fell and crumbled when Junior Moon whacked him into a stupor, tied his hands behind his back and pulled a portable electric razor from beneath his robe.

⌘⌘⌘

Puddin' Pardeaux studied the latest entries in the chintz-covered guest book she had made herself from instructions in Martha Stewart's book: Lance Jones and Vivica Smith, thirteen thirteen South Harbor Boulevard, Anaheim, California, nine two eight zero three. She made a mental note to add the two names to her Christmas card list and went into the kitchen to put the luncheon plates into the dishwasher. As she cleared the table, she noticed the plastic container. *Oh my goodness, they've forgotten the three-bean salad. And after they admired it so.* She grabbed the dish, lifted her keys from the heart-shaped rack next to the back door and whistled for her dog. "Come on, Beau! Let's go for a ride."

She drove slowly, watching for her new friends, and aware of the storm clouds that gathered strength behind her. "Why, Beau, I do believe that that's my corn pudding, and my best Tupperware, sittin' on the side of the road." She eased the car onto the shoulder.

Beau leaped from the back-seat window before the car came to a complete halt and sniffed the ground. He ignored the spilled food. He recognized a hated scent. His body stiffened, and he growled.

"What's the matter, boy? Can you smell them? Are they lost?" Puddin' stepped from her Jeep Cherokee and skidded through a puddle of congealing blood, windmilling her arms for balance. She examined her shoes, then climbed back into the Jeep. She removed the first-aid kit from the glove compartment, placed it on the passenger seat and punched 911 into her cellular phone, reserving the "send" button until she knew what was going on. She put the phone in her lap.

"Find!" she ordered Beau through the window, then slammed the jeep into four-wheel drive and tried to keep up as Beau tore through the brush.

⌘⌘⌘

Wake up, Vivica! Margaret yelled inside Betty/Vivica's head. *Help me out here, Phanny.*

We shall overcome... Phanny sang softly, cowering in Viv's subconscious.

Oh, fiddle-dee-dee, you're useless. Vivica, wake up!

MOONLIGHT BOWL MANIFESTO

Betty, wake up! Oh, whatever the hell your name is, snap out of it. It's General Sherman come to burn down Atlanta.

"Boy, stop messin' with that shaver and help us light up these here torches. It's windier than a bag a farts out here."

"Well, spit shit, Daddy, Momma ruint this hood. She done sewed the holes too little. I can't see squat what I'm doin'."

"If your eyes wasn't restin' so close to your nose, you'd see just fine. Here." Arliss Moon tossed his son a hunting knife and Junior severed the cheap fabric from eyehole to eyehole, nicking the bridge of his nose in the process.

Rick, believing possum-playing to be the better part of valor, moaned but kept his eyes closed when Junior lifted his head up by the hair. The only other human heads Junior had been allowed to shave belonged to Moon cousins infested with lice. As he guided the razor, the wind captured the loosened hair and sailed it into the scrub. After two passes with his Remington, Junior called out to his father and the other BBBs, "Holy Jesus. Look a here. He's turning into a nig—"

A snarling mass of maddened yellow Labrador cut short Junior's speech. Beau was not deceived by concealing robes; he recognized the scent of the human who had shorn his silky coat from his body the year before, causing him chills, insect bites and humiliation. He launched himself at his tormentor and clamped his teeth into the flesh where Junior's hood met his robe. He held on while Junior thrashed and screamed.

Puddin's limb-scratched and stump-battered Jeep crashed into the clearing as Beau launched himself at Junior. She punched "send" and spoke into her phone. "This is Puddin' Pardeaux. I need everybody. Send the whole stationhouse and all the ambulances. It's those flaming crossholes."

"Where are you?" the dispatcher asked.

"I'm at the clearing on the old McWhorter place, off County Road Sixty Four. The one where the teenagers go to party. They got two up on crosses and one on the ground. Beau's got a hold of one of them. Hang on."

Arliss swung at the twisting dog with a dead torch as Junior spun in a circle to loosen Beau's grip by centrifugal force. Beau held on and Junior got dizzy. Puddin' blasted her horn as she bore down upon the BBBs with her truck. Arliss dropped his torch and ran into the woods after his three fleeing cohorts, leaving God to look after his son. A huge gust of wind sent a heavy branch crashing through Puddin's windshield. Her scream distracted Beau, who left his victim and flew to aid his mistress. Junior ran, reeling, into the woods after his father.

As the Big Bad Bubbas ran flat-footed through the trees, a funnel cloud was forming in Baxter County and heading in their direction.

Puddin' awoke to a rough, wet tongue licking her face and a telephone squawking at her. "Hello, hello! Are you all right? Is anybody there? Hello?"

She shook the shattered glass fragments from the phone. "I'm fine. Just a little bump on the head. But I'd 'preciate it if you'd add a tow truck to your list."

"Help's on the way."

"Good. I'm going to see what I can do." Puddin' carefully exited the Jeep Cherokee, carrying her first-aid kit. Beau trotted faithfully behind her until she reached the crosses, then he continued to the far side of the clearing and growled.

"Leave them be, Beau. They've crawled back into their holes by now."

"You're not one of them?"

MOONLIGHT BOWL MANIFESTO

Puddin' jumped at the sound of Rick's voice.

"Good Lord, what happened to your head?" she asked as she untied his hands.

"It's genetic. We've got to help my friends," Rick yelled over the sirens of approaching emergency vehicles. He picked up the abandoned hunting knife and began sawing through the ropes around the chest of the woman he knew only as Betty.

"Unless you want your friend to dive head first into the dirt, you better start on her feet."

By the time the first Emergency Medical Technician arrived, Betty/Vivica was stretched out on the ground in the anti shock position and Puddin' and Rick were gently lowering Lance from the cross.

"Sugar, Sugar, they're gone. It's okay." Puddin' rubbed Vivica/Betty's forearm as the paramedic administered CPR.

"Shut up, Margaret," Vivica squeaked, her eyes flickering.

"Who's Margaret?" the EMT asked.

Puddin' shrugged. "Betty, it's me, Puddin' Pardeaux. You had lunch at my house, remember? You forgot your three-bean salad."

Vivica opened her eyes. She squinted at the flashing red, blue and yellow lights of every squad car, ambulance, fire engine and tow truck in the county. "I've died and gone to Vegas," she croaked.

"She'll be fine. Keep her still and don't let her talk." The EMT peeled and discarded his rubber gloves and snapped on a new pair before moving to Lance's side.

Eight volunteers surrounded Lance's prone form. One raised Lance's head slightly so another could wrap a soft bandage around the gaping, clotted wound in his head. Two others held a board in place so three more could lift his body onto it without injuring him further. Someone held an IV bottle and another, an oxygen tank. Thirty more anguished volunteers milled around. Police officers questioned Rick and Puddin'. Firemen surveyed the area for smoldering torches or flaming crosses. A wrecker driver fastened a chain to the bumper of Puddin's truck. A state trooper ordered everyone to move their vehicles so an ambulance could leave.

Vivica insisted on being loaded into the same ambulance as Lance. "He's my blood brother." She reached for his hand. "Lance, my sweet friend, my love, my heart," she whispered. "Just click those ruby slippers together and tell yourself 'There's no place like home. There's no place like home.'"

⌘⌘⌘

Milton listened to the doctor in amazement, his tape recorder forgotten on the chair next to him. He'd heard the sirens. Almost every volunteer in the county had responded to Puddin's urgent 911 call—all except those on the Moon side of the river.

"This is what happens when a group of people who can't read the back of a Wheaties box interpret the Bible. It's pretty astonishing, really," the doctor continued. "All your friends are going to be all right.

"It was touch and go there for a while for Mr. Cornell. He needed a transfusion, and Mrs. Lakeland insisted it had to be with her blood. Said they made a pact or something when they were kids. We're keeping Mr. Cornell here for a couple of days. Infection, that type of thing. Mrs. Lakeland can go home tomorrow. Mr. Johnson—damndest thing I ever saw, Mr Johnson's scalp—he can leave anytime. Got a minute? I want to show you something."

Milton numbly trailed the doctor into the elevator. "Damndest thing…"—the doctor shook his head—"…that tornado completely passing over West Moon and hitting Moon the way it did." He pressed the button for the basement. "Well, they say those things look for trailer parks. Some kind of magnetic attraction."

Milton followed the white coat from the elevator, down a long corridor through a door marked 'Morgue'. "An act of God, I say." He pulled back the sheet from a body lying on a steel table.

"Was he one of them?" Milt asked as he stared at the lifeless form of Junior Moon.

"Can't prove it, but wouldn't bet against it."

"What is that?" Milton asked about the yellowish white, boomerang-shaped object protruding from Junior's throat.

"Damndest thing, his double-wide not even being close to a farm. The twister had to carry it along for miles, the nearest farm being ten miles…"

"What is it?" Milton interrupted.

"The jawbone of an ass."

⌘⌘⌘

Puddin' knotted the colorful scarf loosely around Betty/Vivica's neck. "There. You look real pretty."

"Thanks, Puddin', but I don't think I'll be allowed to wear it."

"But, it's Laura Ashley." Puddin' looked at Milton expectantly.

"She can wear it 'til her bruises heal."

Puddin' smiled and adjusted the bow, then moved to Lance's bedside and fluffed his pillow.

"Oh, by the way, Puddin'," Betty/Vivica looked at Lance, who nodded his approval, "Lance and I made a mistake when we wrote our address in your guest book. We forgot, we moved. Let me write down our new address."

"And..." Lance prompted, as Puddin' fed him a chocolate.

"...Our real last names," Betty/Vivica finished.

"Why, thank you, Sugar." Puddin' picked up two water pitchers. "I'll just go freshen these up."

After she left the room, Betty/Vivica turned to Lance. "Do you think that was a good idea?"

"Our real names are on our medical charts. Besides, she saved our lives. Anyway, she would have found out about the address eventually."

"How?"

"Sooner or later, everyone goes to Disneyland."

CHAPTER 30
EXPLETIVE DELETED

Marguerite broke a large icicle from the eaves before she entered the barn. "Okay, open the door."

Horace/Harmony scraped the large door over packed snow until the opening was wide enough to admit Marguerite and her glistening sword. "If you hurt one of her animals," he said, following her, "the old lady will have you shot, stuffed and hung over the mantle with the moose head."

"She'll never know. I saw it done in a movie once. I'll shove the icicle through his ear, into his brain. The murder weapon will melt and, *voilá*, she'll think her precious pony died of a stroke."

"All it did was nip you."

"Three fucking times. And it kicked me. I was thinking of shoving this thing up its ass and puncturing its colon, but I'm never going near that end again."

Horace/Harmony pulled the door closed behind him to keep the wind out of the chilly barn. A shaggy Icelandic pony glared at Marguerite as she passed his stall to reach the feed and water. She and Horace had been assigned the care of an assortment of sheep, pygmy goats, and Pepper, the pony from hell.

"You're as full of horseshit as this stall," Horace/Harmony said as he fastened a lead to Pepper's bridle. Pepper nuzzled him affectionately as he led him from his stall. "See," he told Marguerite as he scratched the animal's nose, "he isn't mean; he's just a good judge of character." Horace/Harmony tied the pony's lead to a hand-forged iron loop fixed to the barn siding, picked up a shovel and began removing the evidence of yesterday's meal from the straw-covered stall floor.

"Hey, Horace."

As Horace/Harmony turned at the sound of Marguerite's voice, a frozen fecal missile bounced off his forehead. "Shit!"

"Exactly." Marguerite patted the ewe that had provided her with her ammunition.

Horace/Harmony rubbed his stinging head and, for the first time since they had arrived on the island, thanked God it was winter.

⌘⌘⌘

Hildegarde Knudsen smelled of Avon dusting powder, flour and, faintly, of cinnamon. She was a woman who baked pastries, ate them, and didn't mind if the crust from an apple pie ended up on her hips, or the filling helped round out her *gluteus maximus*. She was comfortable with her body and with her life.

Her husband of forty years, Anders, appeared to have been given more than the usual allotment of bones, causing many of them to stick out at odd angles on his tall, spare body. He smelled of pipe tobacco and wood chips and loved his wife. They had known George Lindstrom since he was a baby, when his family purchased a summer cottage on the island. After his mother and father died only a year apart, a grief-stricken George had sold the cottage to pay off their medical bills. Hildi and Anders promised him he would always have a place with them.

The Knudsen's described their home as small, but elastic; it stretched to fit whomever needed a place to stay. Three compact bedrooms each held two sets of bunk beds with a high, narrow chest of drawers wedged between them. During peak visitation times —family reunions, the Fourth of July, and when the leaves changed colors in the fall—folding cots filled all available floor space. The tiny guest house, Knudsen's Friendly Frog Farm, held an additional set of bunk beds, but appealed more to grubby little boys who didn't mind the absence of a shower or the short walk to the outhouse. Hildi and Anders slept on a sleeper-sofa in the living room, a habit they developed years earlier to discourage teen-aged sleepwalkers. In late spring, summer and early fall, the Knudsen home was often filled with children, grandchildren and family friends. The winters were long and, sometimes, lonely. When George called from California, the Knudsen's were delighted to offer their home as an attitude-adjustment site.

"Aunt Hildi, do you think we should call Medivac?" George was worried. Chelsea Dove lay wrapped in blankets on the couch, her head resting on Hildi's expansive lap.

Hildi set down the spoon she had been using to coax chicken soup between the starving girl's pale lips and glanced at a dusty, framed print of a child with enormous dark eyes by an artist popular twenty-five years earlier. *This baby could have posed for that picture.* She gently smoothed back strands of limp, lackluster hair from Chelsea's colorless cheeks. She sighed. "No. No helicopter. We can't make her go to the hospital. Legally, she's an adult."

"Don't worry, she's fine, Mrs. Knudsen." Ethel/Serene looked up from her one-thousand-piece puzzle. "She told me. She's just conserving energy for her next part." Ethel/Serene hoped her great-grandmother in Florida was as kind as Mrs. Knudsen.

"Mrs. Knudsen!" Marguerite screeched as she yanked

open the sticky back door so hard icicles fell from the eaves, tinkling as they crashed against Hildi's flower boxes. "Mrs. Knudsen!" she screamed again as she slammed the door against a barrage of snowballs. "Horace's trying to kill me!"

Horace/Harmony tumbled through the door after her with a handful of snow to rub in her face.

"Good heavens," Hildi said to George and Anders. "I've got a baby on my lap and children at my back door. It seems the only adult here is working a puzzle on the floor. George, come here and take over." George replaced Hildi on the sofa, placing a pillow on his lap so the harsh denim of his jeans wouldn't chafe Chelsea's sensitive skin.

The crowded back porch of the Knudsen's modest home sheltered a washer and dryer and a bench for sitting while putting on or removing boots. One wall was lined with hooks for coats, scarves and hats; heavy nylon line was strung across a corner to hang wet gloves. Marguerite had learned the hard way not to throw wet woolen mittens into the clothes dryer. Marguerite took off her knit cap; her hair crackled and stood away from her head like a halo in the dry winter air. While she and Horace/Harmony removed their heavy outer garments, Hildi poured them large mugs of steaming cocoa and retrieved stacks of pancakes and a pile of bacon from the oven. Butter, jam and syrup were already on the kitchen table. The rest of them had eaten in an earlier shift.

"Damn, it's colder than a fucking well-digger's ass out there." Marguerite rubbed her hands together vigorously, as if trying to start a fire in her palms. "My fucking fingers are frosted."

Hildegarde clucked. "Do you really have to use language like that?"

MOONLIGHT BOWL MANIFESTO

"What's the matter? You mean the kid?" Marguerite winked at Ethel/Serene. "She's heard the words before. Ask her daddy dearest here."

Ethel/Serene watched Mrs. Knudsen's face carefully, afraid her father had somehow gotten into trouble again.

"It's not Ethel I'm concerned about. She's a smart child, in spite of her parents. She'll figure out what's right."

"Maybe the words are too harsh for your sensitive Midwestern ears," Marguerite suggested.

"Good heavens, no." Hildegarde laughed. "My ancestors were Anglo-Saxon. We invented those words. It's just that you're wasting them."

"Huh?" Marguerite said.

"It's a matter of escalation, Dear."

"You've lost me."

"Sit down. Both of you. Eat your breakfast. I'll explain." Hildegarde poured another mug of cocoa for herself and sat at the table with Marguerite and Horace/Harmony. From his comfortable, worn Barcalounger, Anders chuckled. He had already heard the lecture he knew would follow. George traced the bones of Chelsea's wrist with his index finger. Ethel/Serene, pixie ears alert for grownup talk, pretended to work on her puzzle.

"As I was saying, it's a matter of escalation. Words are weapons, some more powerful than others. Ask Patrick Henry or Thomas Paine. Some words are slingshots, others nuclear bombs."

"Sticks and stones..."

"Please don't interrupt, Marguerite, Dear." Hildegarde sipped her hot drink and continued. "Suppose I were to say things to Mr. Knudsen every day like, 'Anders, Dear, please pass the fucking salt,' or 'Dear, you look like a fucking moron in that shirt?'"

"Then, I guess the words would become harmless. Lose their punch. So what's the big deal about using them?" Marguerite said as she built a tower of buttermilk pancakes on her plate.

Anders smiled behind his hand. Marguerite was taking the bait.

"Okay. Then suppose I get really mad at Mr. Knudsen. So mad I want to hurt him. I want him to know he's the biggest asshole on earth, but I've already called him an asshole everyday of his life."

"Well, I guess maybe you'd have to hit him or something." Marguerite drenched the steaming tower with warm maple syrup and licked her sticky fingers.

"And what if he has an affair with Mrs. Johansen down the street?"

"I guess you'd have to kill him."

"Exactly! And *that's* what's wrong with the world today!"

⌘⌘⌘

Anders entertained his insomnia with eighty-six channels pulled from a satellite, and usually refreshed himself with short naps during the day. The television screen flickered light to dark to light as he prospected the airwaves for old movies. He settled himself into his chair and adjusted the volume on his headset when John Wayne appeared on the Sony.

From her side of the sleeper sofa, his wife smiled at the generosity of a husband willing to give up his bed to a stranger. She tucked the covers around Chelsea's feet on Ander's side of their bed.

Chelsea lay awake in the dark, listening to noises filtered by the night and distilled into sharp-edged clarity. The crystal crunching sound of a foraging animal breaking through a crust of snow hurt her teeth. An icy branch tapping against a window frightened her; then she felt the arm, the warm, soft arm that always seemed to be around her lately. And she slept.

Hildegarde pulled the blanket up to Chelsea's chin with her free arm and watched her breathe. *How did this happen to her? How the fuck did this happen?*

⌘⌘⌘

Ethel/Serene chewed on a strand of hair that had worked itself free from the pipe cleaner Mrs. Knudsen had used to tie it back into a loose ponytail. She concentrated hard on her drawing. Charcoal smudged her fingers, nose and sweatshirt. Her cheek showed remnants of chocolate frosting from the cake she had helped Mrs. Knudsen make that morning, and even the smiling yellow face on her armband wore a chocolate mustache. She was making a birthday present for Chelsea.

The previous year, on Ethel/Serene's sixth birthday, her father asked her if she wanted to pilot their Cessna across the country and free her spirit to frolic with the clouds. She would work through the clouds to become a cloud. Her aura would blend with the rainbow. Ethel/Serene agreed, sure that her father would never do anything to harm her, and excited about the publicity surrounding the proposed journey of enlightenment. Luckily, her mother intervened. Declaring, "There's a fine line between *spirituality* and *fucking nuts*," she packed up her daughter, moved to Reno and sued for divorce. Ethel/Serene settled for a sixth birthday party of carob cake, fruit kebobs and liability waivers.

It was Mrs. Johansen's turn to cuddle Chelsea. All of the neighbors were taking a turn holding, stroking and speaking softly and lovingly to her. They asked nothing in return.

"Why are you doing this? What do you want? Are you an agent?" Chelsea made a feeble attempt to squirm away from Mrs. Johansen's powerful arms. "You smell like a public toilet."

"Yah, that's a good one. Toilet water what smells like a toilet." The cheerful grandmother laughed so heartily, Chelsea's ribs hurt. "Don't tell my grandson," she whispered confidentially. "He gave me this cologne for Christmas. He said it smelled like a Christmas tree." Mrs. Johansen hugged Chelsea closer. "Hildi, I think we better bring this baby to church. She needs to make her peace with God. Tell that heathen husband of yours to warm up the snowmobile."

"She's not going anywhere. The only peace she needs to make is with herself. And don't you call my Anders a heathen."

"I'm sorry. Your Anders is a good man."

"The best." Sigrid Johansen was Hildi's best friend, but she would not allow anyone to suggest her husband was unenlightened.

"Say, Hildi, do you remember that woman from the ferry dock?" Sigrid's and Hildi's little spats were always quickly forgotten. "The one what said you and Anders were going to hell? George, you've got to hear this story."

George looked up from the ancient, well-thumbed *Field and Stream* magazine he had been flipping through. "Uh, oh, Aunt Hildi. What did you do to her?" Their conversation was interrupted briefly as Marguerite, Horace/Harmony and Anders carried in freshly chopped oak for the wood-burning stove.

MOONLIGHT BOWL MANIFESTO

Hildi ladled hot oxtail soup into mugs for each woodchopper and continued her story.

"It was Memorial Day weekend. Anders and I went down to the dock to see if our order from Sears had arrived. Anders had seen these new kinds of hammocks in the catalog..."

"They don't care about hammocks, Honey. Just tell the story." Anders often had to steer the course of a story for his wife.

"Well, they'll certainly care about hammocks if they're still here in the spring."

"You're right, Dear."

"So." Hildi pulled a crumpled tissue from the sleeve of her housedress and delicately patted her nose. She tucked the tissue away and continued. "Anders and I were down at the dock when we saw Olav Svensen backing a van down the ferry ramp for some tourists."

"Olav Svenson?" Marguerite asked.

"He works for the ferry captain, hiking cars." Hilda said. "The last time a tourist tried to back a van down the ramp himself ...well, let's just say the F in Ford doesn't stand for float. Anyway, to continue my story, we noticed a sign on the side of the van that read: New Christians, Sleepy Hollow, Illinois. Anders thought they were that famous singing group, the one that was always so perky and cheerful, and we waited around to get their autographs." Anders nodded. "Finally, a well-dressed, silver-haired lady comes over to the van. Anders and I say hello and he tells her how much he liked her song, you know, the one that goes 'Green, green. It's green they say, on the far side of the hills...'

"Well, she gets kind of huffy. She tells us that that was The New Christy Minstrels, not The New Christians and asks us out of the blue if we were born again. Well, you know Anders. He tells her he has been born thirty-four times, but each time had the good sense to die first. For some reason, this seems to set the lady off, and that's when she told us that we were going to hell, and Anders tells her that after a winter on the island, hell might be a nice warm place. Then she tells us that, unless we recognize Jesus Christ as our own personal savior, we'll never see the kingdom of heaven. So, of course, Anders tells her that, as he never met the man, he wouldn't know Jesus from Jell-O."

Hildi finally took a breath. "Anders, Dear, do you want to finish the story?"

"You're doing fine."

"By now, the rest of the New Christians had finished taking pictures of seagulls and found the van. They were smiling at us, but I swear, the corners of their mouths were twitching with the effort. I felt like we were being measured for pitchforks and cloven hooves. I believe in God. And Anders, some days he does, and some days he doesn't, but he's still the most moral person I know and that's exactly what I told those so-called Christians. Anders says that, if there is a God, he'll judge people by who they are, not who they condemn. What's the quote you used, Dear, the one that made the lady call you a communist?"

"'My atheism, like that of Spinoza, is true piety towards the universe and denies only gods fashioned by men in their own image, to be servants of their human interests.'"

"That's it. By Carlos Santana."

"George Santayana."

"That must have shut them up." Marguerite finished her soup and sucked noisily on an oxtail bone.

"Hardly. She said that only a religious person could be

moral and all the other Christians started 'amening' and praising the Lord. I told her that that was the most ridiculous thing I had ever heard. She said that if there was no fear of eternal damnation, there was no reason to behave morally. Then, what was it you said to her, Dear?"

"I asked her what kind of religious person only behaves morally because he fears punishment. Shouldn't a person be good because it's the right thing to do? 'By your logic,' I told her, 'the non-religious person would have more reason to be moral, believing he would be judged here on earth with no chance for another shot. That's social morality. A religious person can sin his whole life, repent, and spend eternity cloud-surfing with the angels. To me, that's hypocritical morality.'"

"What did she say to that?" George had spent many a pleasurable evening being argued into a theological corner by Anders.

"She put herself on automatic pilot and began spouting Bible verses. You can't argue with a robot."

"Come on, Anders. You don't quit so easily."

"They weren't worth my breath, George; although I did leave them with a quote from George Bernard Shaw: '...what you fellows don't understand is that you must get at a man through his own religion and not through yours.'"

"'Religion is the opium of the people.' Karl Marx. The real truth is in the stars and planets." Horace/Harmony said.

"And who is it what made those stars and planets?" Sigrid defended her version of God.

Chelsea smiled. She was enjoying the discussion. People were arguing, but no one was angry. She liked Sigrid, with the big, booming voice and Norwegian accent, and all the others who sat with her and nurtured her. What she couldn't understand was why they did it. They asked nothing from her. She knew they would be pleased if she ate, but no one was upset with her when she didn't. Maybe it had something to do with this religion thing.

"As children, many of us had invisible playmates," Anders said. Most of those in the room nodded and smiled. Horace/Harmony's eyes brightened with moisture as he recalled painful sessions in a therapist's office expunging his imaginary best friend, Buzzy. "Some people like to say that these playmates were guardian angels," Anders went on. "As adults, some of us still have an invisible friend. Only now we like to call him God. This way, people don't say we're nuts."

"Religion is for people who can't afford a therapist."

"Now, Horace, don't be so hard on the world. If some folks find comfort in God, let them have him. I'd like to think of God as a good parent. He's always there if you need him. However, he doesn't require you to have dinner at his house every Sunday night for the rest of your life."

"What do you believe in, Anders?"

"I believe in the Golden Rule. I'll be happy if my epitaph reads:

> *Here lies a moral man*
> *Who had a pleasant life.*
> *He left God to those who needed him,*
> *And died before his wife.*

At the sound of snowmobiles and barking dogs, Ethel/Serene ran to the window. "Mrs. Knudsen, they're back from the Mercantile." Two Easter escorts carrying paper grocery sacks burst through the back door, dumped the bags on the kitchen table and huddled as close as they could to the wood-burning stove without bursting into flames. "Can we have the surprise now?" Ethel/Serene whispered into Mrs. Knudsen's ear."

"Yes, Dear."

"Come on, Daddy, you can help." Ethel/Serene grabbed Horace/Harmony's hand and led him to the back porch, where the cake was hidden. Mrs. Knudsen followed with the bag containing candles and ice cream.

Horace/Harmony watched his daughter poke pink-striped candles into the peanut butter-walnut fudge cake. He disapproved of sugar and fat, but hadn't had much to say about Ethel/Serene's diet since they left California. She looked healthy enough; her cheeks were red and chapped from hours of playing in the snow and cold; her eyes were bright with excitement.

"Daddy, you light the candles and carry the cake. Mrs. Knudsen will bring the ice cream. I'll turn out the lights."

In the dark, as instructed, everyone in the living room but Chelsea donned paper party hats. Chelsea, having forgotten it was her birthday, assumed ice had snapped another power line and waited patiently for Anders to light the emergency oil lanterns.

"Happy birthday to you..." Ethel/Serene sang as twenty-eight candles floated mysteriously from the kitchen into the living room.

As Chelsea's eyes adjusted to the dark, she saw the cake, and the pointy hats and silly grins on everyone assembled. Only when Mrs. Johansen handed her a hat imprinted with the words *Birthday Girl*, and kissed her on the cheek did she understand that the celebration was for her.

"Happy birthday to you..." the rest joined in.

"Hey, Slats!" Marguerite yelled when the song ended and the lights were turned on. "Congratulations. I didn't think you'd make it to your birthday."

Hildegarde passed around plates of cake with generous scoops of ice cream along side.

"I'll have two dishes, please," Ethel/Serene told Mrs. Knudsen. "I'll bring Chelsea hers." When Mrs. Knudsen shook her head, Ethel/Serene reassured her. "Oh, I know she'll eat her very own birthday cake."

Ethel/Serene's good intentions were no match for two overflowing plates, and, as she turned to hand Chelsea her share, two lumps of fudge ripple slid down two chocolate slopes, off two plates and onto the bearskin rug. Ethel/Serene froze, her eyes begged her father to believe it was an accident. George, remembering the pizza incident in Chicago, watched Horace/Harmony carefully.

"Well, you silly girl." Horace/Harmony winked at his daughter. "This bear won't eat. He's hibernating. Let's give his share to the dogs. Mrs. Knudsen, I think these plates need refilling."

Ethel/Serene was disappointed when Chelsea didn't touch her dish. "Mrs. Knudsen, may I give Chelsea her birthday present now?"

"Yes, Dear."

Chelsea stared at the portrait Ethel/Serene handed her. It was a skull with long, flowing hair.

"It's you," the young artist said proudly. "Can you tell?"

"Looks exactly like you," Marguerite offered.

"It's uncanny," George added.

"Please don't cry." Ethel/Serene patted Chelsea's wet

cheek. "I can't draw tears."

Chelsea pulled the child to her, and Mrs. Johansen's ample arms easily circled both of them.

"Mrs. Knudsen," Chelsea asked. "If it's no trouble, I think I might like a tiny bowl of soup."

⌘⌘⌘

The following Sunday, with Horace/Harmony's permission, Hildi took Ethel/Serene with her to The Little White Church of the Laughing Jesus.

BARBARA JONES

CHAPTER 31

JUST DON'T INHALE

Nana Cornell sat on the edge of Lance's pool, her thickly-veined bare feet stirring the water at the shallow end. She lifted her legs to avoid the pool sweep and noticed her toenails needed clipping. She'd clip them later, after Irwin's broadcast. She tipped her face toward the sun and closed her eyes, smiling at the warmth on her cheeks. Before the warmth could turn to burn, Rusty's joyous yapping reminded her that it was time to feed the neighbor's bulldog.

"All right, I'm coming." Nana Cornell dried her feet carefully and rolled down the legs of her elastic-waisted, polyester-blend slacks. Coot Court had decreed that seniors were allowed to wear this more maneuverable attire. Her sixties-vintage bowling shirt read Grey's Groceries Groovy Grannies.

Rusty and Goty faced each other across the electronic no man's land that separated their two yards. For five seconds they froze, then broke and tore madly parallel down the perimeter until a warning buzz turned them to race madly back to the starting point.

"You can play later, boys," Nana told the dogs as she crossed into Horace/Harmony's yard. "Right now, Goty has to eat and I've got to check Horace's mail."

The hungry bulldog trotted after the old lady into his master's kitchen while the young pup barked a challenge from his side of the invisible fence.

While Lance's grandmother hummed along with the whirring can-opener, strings of drool dangled briefly from Goty's jowls, then stretched and dripped to the floor. When she placed the bowl of food on the floor, the dog sniffed, snorted and finally ate the artichoke hearts she had opened for him. Since she misplaced her glasses, Goty had been fed canned beets, baked beans and cream of broccoli soup. She rinsed the can, threw it in the recycling bin and opened the front door to greet the mail carrier.

"Good afternoon, Mrs. Cornell. Any word from the Brights?" The mailman handed her Horace/Harmony's mail. Delivery had become much more reliable after Irwin announced that all postal carriers must introduce themselves to the people on their routes. Since they now had faces to go with the names on Social Security checks, tax refunds and birthday cards, fewer carriers had been dumping mail into sewers to lighten their loads.

"Not a one, Myron. They must be having too much fun to write. You might as well give me Lance's mail, too, and Velma's."

"They're really keeping you busy, taking care of three houses like you are, Mrs. Cornell."

"Oh, pish, Myron. I'm loving every minute of it. You have a good afternoon now."

Nana Cornell took all of the mail with her back to Lance's house. She'd sort through it later when she found her glasses.

⌘⌘⌘

Irwin's nightly broadcast had ascended the ratings charts to become the number-one rated show on the planet. For fairness, Irwin alternated local radio and television stations, and he permitted no commercial breaks. Any station that wished was allowed, even encouraged, to pick up his signal. He had no standard format. Some evenings he introduced new rules, such as the one requiring anyone working in an elder-care facility to read a biography of each patient before giving care; or the law that said teenagers must work part time at a nursing home before they received a driver's license so they might understand that the old lady in the car in front of them might not have as quick a reaction time as they did. Another popular, high-pledge-producing edict ordered automobile design engineers to work for an auto mechanic for six months before being allowed to design a car. They would also be forced to listen to the complaints of customers about high labor costs incurred because of designs like the one that required a mechanic to lift the engine from the engine mount to replace the last two sparkplugs. Some evenings he expounded on one of his theories: "The world has technologically and legally become so complex, the whole world has reached its Peter Principle. We have reached our level of incompetency." Or, "Every body is allotted a certain amount of illness that must be used up—if you've been healthy your whole life, you will probably drop dead suddenly of a massive heart attack." Or, "The U.S. Government is a giant condo association, and taxes are your dues." Once, he even held a contest to find a better expression than "Have a nice day," but canceled it when most of the entries started with "Go" and ended with "yourself."

    Buttons, bumper stickers and coffee mugs blazoned with Schwepisms appeared on lapels, cars and desks like mushrooms after a spring rain: "Stupid people don't ask questions." "It's not dysfunction, it's life." "The soul is the security deposit for your piece of earth." "That's why it's called an accident." Irwin was astounded by the response to his ramblings. Promotional offers had been pouring in. California didn't seem to understand that it was under siege.

    "Hi, neighbors, it's me, Irwin," he started his broadcast as usual. "Who have you visited today?" Irwin sat on the edge of the stage at the Self Center. His feet dangled, his belly rested comfortably on his lap. Behind him, Bambi bumped and scraped an easel across the floor. She gripped a pointer under her chin and clasped poster boards in her left armpit. Although the Center was equipped with millions of dollars of multi-media equipment capable of creating computer graphics, interactive presentations and virtual reality dog-and-pony shows, Irwin preferred a wooden easel and hand-drawn visual aids for his lectures. He told his audience simple props kept him connected to reality, but the truth was he enjoyed the peace and quiet for a few hours every morning while Bambi designed the day's inspirational images.

Bambi had gained a grudging respect for her husband and a reflected notoriety for herself. She didn't understand what all the fuss was over Irwin and knew that anyone who saw him in his underwear couldn't possibly take him seriously, but as long as he stayed clothed, she'd gladly bow in his limelight. She set the day's posters in order on the easel, hung the pointer from the crosspiece and backed into the wings before the camera could pick up her naked face—the hostages were not allowed makeup, and Irwin would not make an exception for his wife.

Irwin struggled to his feet, his knee joints protesting noisily. He turned away from the camera briefly to pull up the zipper that had fled from his waistband when he sat down. Unabashed, he picked up the pointer and tapped the two words appearing on the first poster: DO DAD.

Leon smacked the heel of his hand against his forehead. "Oh, Christ, he's really going to do it. Operation Do Dad! It was supposed to be a joke, that's all." He rested his elbows on the desk and leaned his head heavily on his palms. "I wish George and Miltie were back. I can't handle him alone. And these pledges ...we're getting them in yen, colones, Deutsche marks, rupees..."

MOONLIGHT BOWL MANIFESTO

"More of the same?" Marge asked as she and Leon watched Irwin on a monitor in an office near the auditorium.

Leon nodded. Pledges, checks and money orders had not slackened since the Really Big Night of Stars. Unfortunately, the tone of the requests accompanying many of the pledges had changed. A middle-aged divorced woman from Toad Suck, Arkansas, promised a million dollars if all men dumping their wives for younger women were castrated. An athletic shoe executive from China was willing to give twenty-five million American dollars if California would stop harping against child labor and about human rights. Those callers willing to donate to a noble social experiment grew fewer and those wanting their pound of flesh grew daily.

Irwin lifted the first poster by a corner and sailed it into the audience. He thumped the second sign with the thick end of the pointer, knocking over the easel. "Never mind, it's an easy message to remember." He bent to pick up the sign and felt his zipper slide southward again. Using the poster to cover his move, he zipped his pants, then raised the sign and held it against his chest. "Do Drugs And Die."

"Shit." Leon lowered his head to the desk.

"What the hell's he doing?"

"George!" Leon stood to embrace his friend. "Thank God you're back. He's launching Operation Do Dad."

"But, that was a joke. We were just goofin'."

"He ain't laughing."

⌘⌘⌘

In the Oval Office, the President sat up straight in his chair, raised the volume on his television set and spoke into the phone, "Get in here."

⌘⌘⌘

Horace/Harmony cupped the warm, smooth mug of decaf mocha cappuccino supreme eight inches under his nose and let the fragrant steam caress his nostrils. He had found a ten-dollar bill in his jeans pocket and a farewell note from Mrs. Knudsen telling him, "Buy yourself something nice when you get back home." The money covered his coffee and a chocolate biscotti for Ethel/Serene, but left nothing for a tip. He waited until the server was busy with another customer, threw the ten on the table, grabbed his daughter's hand and fled the coffee bar. He ducked into the electronics store next door and melted anonymously into a polyester and denim sea of shoppers. A bank of television sets, all tuned to the same station, caught his attention. From every screen, Irwin Schwep looked back at him, and from every speaker, Irwin's voice froze shoppers mid-browse. "Do Drugs and Die."

Ethel/Serene tugged on her father's hand. "Puhlease, Daddy, can we go home now? I want to see Goty." The child, tired from their long journey home, crossed her legs and sat on the showroom floor at her father's feet. It had been fun to watch her dad kiss the ground when they landed back in California, but a little sad when they said good-bye to their new Wisconsin friends. However, Marguerite said she'd do lunch with her soon, and George assured her he'd make the funny lady keep that promise. Chelsea, who Mrs. Knudsen had insisted in keeping on the island until she gained twenty pounds, swore she would also visit when she returned home. Ethel/Serene didn't mind Horace/Harmony stopping at the mall for a "civilized" cup of coffee on the way home, but now that she was so close, she couldn't wait to see her dog and sleep in her non-custodial-parent-house bed.

"Soon, Sweetie." Horace/Harmony lifted Ethel/Serene and sat her in a black leather vibrating chair. "You wait here a minute. Don't talk to anyone. Don't sign anything."

He pushed through the crowd, looking for a naked upper arm. "You, Easter," he asked the nearest man without an armband. "I just got back from camp. What's he talking about?"

"You got me, Nate." The Easter smiled and stuck out his hand. "I'm Bob. Glad to meet you. Let's watch this thing together."

"Yeah, yeah." Horace/Harmony quickly clasped, then released the proffered hand, not wanting to get a citation for unfriendliness. Ten citations meant a visit to Coot Court and a possible reassignment to camp. He returned his attention to multiple Irwins warning him from the television screens.

"Do Drugs and Die." Irwin paused, believing profundities should be given time to sink in. "For some time, boys and girls, we've been intercepting illegal drug shipments to the state of California and seizing marijuana crops from the happy farmers in the mountains. Instead of destroying these stockpiles as usual, we have decided to distribute them."

Cheers erupted from the audience at the Center. Irwin waited for silence.

"However, and here's the funny part, we've infused this supply with a deadly, quick-acting poison."

"Shit, shit, shit." Leon pounded the desk three times. Marge gasped.

"This isn't fun anymore." George shook his head.

"It's very simple," Irwin continued. "Starting next week, we're funneling these tainted drugs through usual channels: on the street, in executive bathrooms, at rock concerts, on playgrounds. We're also opening free drug rehab centers. It's your choice. Kick the habit or kick the bucket. We launch operation Do Dad tomorrow. Volunteers will flood your neighborhoods with posters warning of the danger and listing the addresses of hospitals and rehab centers. They'll go door to door, alley to alley, school to school. Any drug you can ingest, we can poison. Oh sure, there'll be clean drugs out there somewhere; but, can you trust your dealer? Can he trust his?"

Irwin ended his broadcast with his usual admonition, "*Nolite exspoliare facultatem.*"

⌘⌘⌘

In the Oval Office the President turned to the agent. "Bring him here."

⌘⌘⌘

Horace/Harmony raced up the front walk to his house. His chest was dry and tight. His lungs burned from the exertion of running from the bus stop. Ethel/Serene slid from his arms as he punched in the security code. When the door opened, a joyous bulldog tangled himself in his master's legs and yelped at the unexpected kick to his ribs when Horace/Harmony tripped over him and dashed up the stairs to his bedroom. Ethel/Serene bent to receive welcoming kisses from Goty.

Five minutes, and a frantic search later, Horace/Harmony pounded on Lance Cornell's back door, summoning the old woman who was supposed to be watching his house.

"Oh, Horace. How nice to see you back," Nana Cornell greeted her neighbor. "I've got some mail for you. Why, what's the matter, Dear? You're all out of breath."

"Mrs. Cornell..." he panted, "...the white powder in the crystal bowl on my bedroom bureau..." He leaned against the patio door to catch his breath. "What did you do with it?"

"Oh, yes, Dear," the nearsighted old lady answered. "The potpourri. It was stale. It had no more smell. I flushed it."

⌘⌘⌘

Crossing and uncrossing his legs, Irwin sipped nervously from a glass of ice water. He had visited the White House many years earlier, when he won his junior-high school science fair and received a certificate and a handshake from the Vice President, but he had never been in the Oval Office before. Settling on the legs-crossed position, he unconsciously tapped his right foot against the underside of the coffee table as he listened to his commander in chief.

"Thank you for coming, Irwin." Forgoing his desk in favor of a less intimidating seating arrangement, the President sat across from Irwin on one of two facing sofas.

"You're welcome, Sir." Irwin tried a smile, but could only manage a quick twitch of the lips. Struck shy by the power of the White House and the greatness of his own humility, none of Irwin's muscles were functioning at peak capacity. He assumed he had been sent for to receive some sort of honor, maybe a plaque, or even, as Bambi dared suggest, The Congressional Medal of Honor. At the very least, he supposed the President wanted his advice on implementing his theories nationally.

"It's over, Irwin. Me, and the boys in Congress, were hoping you could pull it off, but it just didn't fly."

"Sir?" Irwin was confused. These didn't sound like the opening remarks of a medal presentation.

"Hell, the whole world was pulling for you. Well, of

course, we got some flak from the garment workers unions and the diet industry folks, but nothing we couldn't divert or subsidize."

"I don't understand. I..."

"And the old people and fat people love you. You know how many old, fat voters there are in this country, Irwin?" The President patted his own considerable paunch. "I even thought of naming you my running mate in the next election."

Irwin brightened at this revelation, although he'd rather join Weight Watchers than run as a Republican.

"Then you came up with this." The President slid a file marked Top Secret across the table to Irwin.

As Irwin reached for the bright red folder, his leg convulsed and kicked the table, spilling a pitcher of water and ice cubes and soaking the file. Humiliation bloomed in his cheeks as he dabbed at the mess with his shirttail.

"Never mind that, Irwin. You know what's in the report. It's operation Do Dad." The President slid down the couch to avoid the dripping water.

Irwin tucked his cold, wet shirt into his pants. "But, Sir, Do Drugs and Die is a good campaign. It gets rid of drug-connected crime, saves children, mothers, babies..."

"Schwep," the President interrupted. "You can't go around killing off American citizens for misdemeanors."

"But, the pushers, the gangs..."

"Forget it. You're done. We're taking back California."

"You can't," Schwep blustered. "I've still got General Sherman—and the Center. I'll...I'll forget operation Do Dad. You don't really want California back. Give me another chance." Irwin pushed back the glasses that slid down his sweaty nose.

"Listen, Irwin, you tried. The kid's been grounded long

MOONLIGHT BOWL MANIFESTO

enough."

"General Sherman," Irwin muttered, running his hands through his hair and pulling at the roots. "I'll disintegrate it. Just like the fences."

The President tossed Irwin a folder marked *Offence*. "We know how you did it. We know all about you, Winnie. There's no secret weapon. You soaked those little trees, just like the fences. We knew General Sherman was a bluff."

"Then why did you let us?"

"The world's circling the rim of a moral toilet." The leader of the free world swirled his index finger through a puddle of ice water on the table. "Following the rules, I can do little more than watch our country get flushed down the crapper." He slapped the puddle and splashed water over the rosewood surface. "You had some good, if politically incorrect, ideas that might have helped bring us together. Everyone seemed to be on your side, so I looked the other way."

"But now?"

"Nobody likes you anymore."

Irwin focused on an ice cube melting into the expensive oriental carpet, wishing he could do the same.

"Oh, and Schwep, before you go..." The President stood, cueing Irwin to rise. "What the hell does it mean?" He put his arm around Irwin's shoulder and guided him firmly toward the door.

"Sir?"

"The Latin. Your motto. The way you sign-off your broadcast."

"*Nolite exspoliare facultatem.*"

"That's it. What's it mean?"

"Don't screw up a good thing."

⌘⌘⌘

"Do you think he bought it?" The director of the CIA asked his boss later that day.

"Of course he did," the President replied. "He's a patriotic American and a brilliant chemist, but he'd never understand. You can't fuck with a drug economy."

The South American drug lord nodded. "You should have just killed him."

The President slammed his fist on his desk. "Listen up, Juan Carlos, this is The United States of America. We don't do things like that here."

⌘⌘⌘

Irwin rowed until his elbows ached and blisters dotted his palms. When he could no longer see land and was certain the shore was too far away for him to swim back, he lifted the oars from their locks and threw them overboard. Then he unscrewed the top of a gallon thermos and saturated the bottom and sides of the wooden boat with Offence. From a blue and white cooler, he retrieved a baloney and cheese sandwich and a Classic Coke. He found his place in a dog-eared copy of an Aldous Huxley novel, munched his lunch and waited.

CHAPTER 32

WHERE IS MICHAEL CAINE WHEN YOU NEED HIM?

Milton kept his eyes on the flight attendant. His hands gripped the armrests tightly, his spine stiffened in its full and upright position, and his buttocks clenched as if suction alone would keep the plane in the air. His shoulders and neck ached with the effort of keeping the jet flying, but he knew if he relaxed his vigilance for an instant, they would all plummet to a fiery death. Although a fast peek to the left assured him the wings were still intact, he whipped his head back to watch for any telltale change in expression on the flight attendant's face. She smiled professionally as she handed out drinks and Milton's sphincter relaxed sufficiently to allow a release of the gasses trapped in his intestines.

"Hey, big guy, take it easy." Rick Johnson sat down in the aisle seat next to Milton, adjusted the fresh-air valve overhead and punched Milton's thigh. "In a few hours, we'll be home-sweet-home. Or, anyway, you'll be home. I'll still be a hostage."

"I don't have a home. Marge, me and the kids, we live at the Center. Before that, we lived in our car."

"What about after? I mean, you are going to let us go sometime?"

"Yeah, I guess. Of course. Sure. Pretty soon, I bet." His voice trailed off. "I hope."

"I got it!" Rick pummeled the seatback in front of him. Milt looked out of the window, sure Rick's pounding had loosened a wing. "After this is all over, you can work for me. You can be my head bodyguard."

"I didn't do a very good job guarding your body at the Center, when you almost hanged yourself, or in Moon, when the BBB tried to re-style your hair." Milt looked at the path of hairless scalp dividing Rick Johnson's head into eastern and western hemispheres.

Rock and Roll's newest poster boy for testosterone poisoning unconsciously patted the surgical dressing covering the stitches at the base of his skull. "You didn't work for me then. Come on. You'll be great."

"Well, you certainly seem to need looking after. But, don't you already have a chief of security?"

"I'll buy him off."

"You can't just buy people, Rick. Remember, we talked about that. A man needs to work."

"Okay. First I'll apologize to him, then I'll pay him off. Better yet, I'll get someone to produce his screenplay."

"Your bodyguard writes screenplays?"

"So do my chauffeur, my hairdresser and my pool boy."

"Is it any good? Does he know what he's doing?"

"It doesn't make any difference. I know producers. And who you know is a lot more important than what you know, unless what you know is about who you know. You know?"

"I guess so. If you think it will be okay..."

Rick stuck out his hand. "Deal?"

Milton loosened his bloodless fingers from the right armrest and reached for his new employer's hand, but before contact was made the plane lurched and Milton convulsively re-grasped the armrest. "Mother of God! What was that?"

"Relax. It's just a little turbulence. Have we got a deal?"

Milton nodded, but kept his hands where they were.

MOONLIGHT BOWL MANIFESTO

Betty/Vivica gingerly handed the full airsickness bag to the flight attendant who exchanged it for an Alka Seltzer and a glass of water.

"You never get airsick," Lance accused her.

She dropped two large, white tablets into the glass and watched the water fizz for a moment before she answered him. "I've never had three helpings of corn pudding, three-bean salad and fried okra before flying before." She held her nose and drank the bubbling liquid. "Damn you, Margaret Mitchell."

"Don't blame Margaret. I think you're starting to like southern food."

"Don't be..." a tremendous belch interrupted her denial, "...ridiculous."

"We need our strength to recuperate from our injuries," Margaret said. "If I didn't feed us, we'd starve. Vivica eats like a skinny bird and Phanny's on a hunger strike until the world can all live as brothers."

"Now, there's a real sacrifice," Lance said. "Next, she'll hold her breath 'til you turn blue."

"Good afternoon," a voice came over the public address system. "This is your captain speaking. We are experiencing some slight mechanical irregularities, and for your safety, I have turned on the seat belt sign."

"Hey, Velma." Lance reached over and tickled the stockinged foot sticking out into the aisle. "Wake up, gorgeous, it's happy hour."

While Velma/Veronica rubbed the blanket creases from her cheeks and tried to scrape hangover fuzz off her tongue with her teeth, Lance turned back to Betty/Vivica. "What's the biggest cause of plane crashes?"

"Knock it off, you jerk. This could be serious."

199

"Come on, Viv. What causes most plane crashes?"
"Pilot error?"
"Gravity."
"You're such a villain."

Rick snapped the metal ends of his belt together and studied Milt's stony profile. He had never seen a man that white. His new bodyguard was clenching his jaw so tightly, Rick expected to see a bitten-off tongue tip or shattered teeth fly out of his mouth at any second.

"This is your captain again. I'm afraid our mechanical irregularity has become more serious."

Milton sucked in his underwear with his behind.

"I'm going to attempt a landing. Please follow the flight attendant's instructions."

"Hail Mary a cab," cried Milton. "We're going down."

The crippled plane ripped jagged pathways through unsuspecting clouds as the pilot fought the gods for control. An explosion in the tail section rocked and twisted the plane as shrapnel sheared nuts from bolts, welds snapped and electrical connections pulled free or shorted out. Sprung oxygen masks dangled like giant yellow insects over panicked passengers, their heads buried in pillows on their laps. Way too fast, landing wheels touched the earth, then folded under the plane, exposing the fuselage to the impact. As the sliding belly plowed a furrow through the open countryside, seams opened, hoses split and noxious fluids splashed and sprayed the cabin and cockpit. For lack of enough remaining equipment to take it any farther, the plane finally stopped short, a sharp list to the left flinging luggage, blankets and safety gear from overhead bins.

Lance, Margaret Mitchell and the Widow Lakeland were the first to recover enough to unbuckle themselves.

MOONLIGHT BOWL MANIFESTO

"Y'all look for the flight attendant. I'll check on the others." Margaret said.

"Margaret? Where's Viv?" Lance's injured arm throbbed. He needed his best friend, not some southern psychotic manifestation of early childhood trauma.

"She's dead. Phanny's okay though. Hurry, we've got to get these people out of here."

Stunned and confused by the news of Betty/Vivica's death, Lance obeyed Margaret's command and soon located the flight attendant under a pile of blankets. He helped her to an exit where she deployed the emergency slide. Acrid smoke was rapidly filling the cabin, but groans, prayers and obscenities made locating victims easy. Lance herded them all toward the exit and was relieved to see the pilot stagger out of the cockpit door, hat askew, captain's wings hanging defiantly from his torn jacket. His co-pilot followed.

"Out, out, out!" Margaret ordered her dazed and bruised fellow travelers as she pushed them out the door, ignoring the flight attendant's attempts to take charge. "Run when you hit the ground. Get away from the plane. Walk if you can't run. Crawl if you can't walk."

Milton, surprised to be alive, pushed a heavy piece of carry-on luggage off his lap, released his seat belt, wiggled his toes and was pleased to discover his legs were still attached to his body. Next to him, Rick Johnson sat quietly, leaning forward, his face still pressed into a protective pillow. Milton poked him playfully. "Hey, you old horny toad, we better get out of here." When he received no response, Milt gently lifted Rick by the shoulders until he was sitting upright. His friend's head fell forward and bright crimson drops fell onto the light blue pillowcase. "Oh Christ, oh God, oh Christ. I've done it to you again." Milt ripped the cover from his own pillow and held it against the four-inch gash on the right side of Rick's head. "I let you get hurt." He tried to lift the bleeding superstar, but was stopped by the fastened seat belt. Adrenaline pumped. He yanked the restraint free from its anchor, picked up Rick, and charged toward the exit, stumbling over a bloody fire extinguisher on the way. At the door he argued briefly with Margaret and the captain about who should be the last to leave the plane. The argument was settled when an explosion blew the four of them out the door and down the inflatable ramp.

The bedraggled little band of survivors re-grouped about fifty yards from the downed aircraft to assess their injuries and count noses. Milton cradled Rick's still body is his arms while Margaret checked for vital signs.

"Where the hell are we?" Velma/Veronica picked a honey-coated almond from her hair, examined it and popped it into her mouth. "There's nothing here but scenery."

"Some big square state." Lance shaded his eyes with his hand and surveyed their surroundings, his broken left arm hanging limply against his side. As far as he could see in two directions was open land covered with scrubby brush and scattered, stunted trees. To the east blue-gray mountains loomed, patched with green and tipped with white. To the north, only a football-field's length in front of the burning jet, a massive ridge jutted from the sloping earth, hiding whatever was behind it. Lance watched a tumbleweed cartwheel by. "I think we're on the Ponderosa."

"I can't find a pulse." Margaret held two fingers against the injured man's throat.

"You've got to help him," Milton pleaded. "This wasn't supposed to happen. The whole thing was a joke," Milton rasped, his voice husky with smoke and emotion. "A big, fucking joke."

"Try listening for breath sounds," Phanny told Margaret. "That's what we did at Woodstock."

Margaret leaned close, putting her ear next to Rick's mouth and nose. She listened, then abruptly cupped her breast with her hand, leaned back and slapped him across the face. "Why, fiddledy-dee, that rascal pinched my bosom."

"That's what they did at Woodstock," Phanny said.

All twelve people on board survived the crash, including four Easter escorts and the crew—fourteen, if you included Phanny and Margaret, thirteen, if you believed that Betty/Vivica was really dead. Lance preferred to believe she had merely retreated to a safe corner of her psyche until the crisis was over. Milton, after saying a prayer thanking St. Jude that Rick would be okay, wondered if he really wanted a job as bodyguard for the horniest, most accident-prone superstar alive. Maybe eating crow and moving back to New York wasn't really such a bad idea. He might even attend the mall college that advertised so heavily during daytime talk shows. He was picturing himself as a highly paid computer programmer when all the hairs on the back of his neck stood up. Someone was watching them.

Out of the corner of her eye, Margaret thought she saw a figure standing on the ridge, but when she looked again, there was nothing there. She moved closer to Milt and noticed the rest of her group pulling themselves into a protective huddle with Milt at the quarterback position. No one could say what had frightened them until a squeak from Betty/Velma directed their collective gaze northward.

They stood in tableau on the ridge—a thousand warriors, shoulder to shoulder in the front line, behind them legions more. They wore jeans torn so short pocket linings and tanned behinds hung below the ragged edges. Shirtsleeves were ripped off or rolled to the shoulder. Bare feet poked out of split and rotted sneakers. The men were unshaven and wore their filthy, knotted hair loose or tied back with colorful bandanas. Many of the women wore braids pierced with feathers and tied with denim thread. Their plant-stained faces glowed bright yellow, and their eyes burned with avarice as they appraised the twelve fresh disaster victims. Their lips were dyed black and the corners of their mouths extended in curved lines to emulate the grinning icon on their armbands. Their arms were extended at chest height and each held, shield-like, a yellow, lined legal pad in the left hand, and a pen, sword-like, in the right.

The chant began softly, a soothing sound of polite party conversation swirling through a room. "Sue, sue, sue." Soon the intensity grew to that of an annoying television commercial until each word was enunciated clearly. "Sue, sue, sue." Finally, the words resounded like the voice of a television evangelist. "Sue, sue, sue!" The warriors raised their swords and shields above their heads then lowered them. Then silence.

"What are they doing?" Milton whispered.

"Don't worry," Rick said. "I saw this in a movie once. They're saluting us for our bravery. Now they'll turn and disappear over the ridge."

The barbarians didn't move.

"Father!" Betty/Vivica, shocked back to consciousness, screamed when she saw the pig's head. It stared at her sightlessly from a stake held by one of the savages.

"Viv! You're alive." Lance rejoiced, temporarily.

"Shut up," Rick hissed. "This is supposed to be silent homage."

MOONLIGHT BOWL MANIFESTO

"Mother, it's Father." Betty/Vivica mouthed the words.

It was, indeed, Veronica Lakeland's late husband, for when the last trainload of lawyers pulled away from the California railroad station, the portly Hamilton Lakeland had been foraging in the supply car. He was rummaging through an overturned dumpster next to the tracks when a sound reminiscent of his litter days drew him to the train. While the call wasn't exactly the "sooiee" the farmer used to announce dinner, it was close enough for him to expect food.

Milton drew circles with his toe in the dry earth and waited for divine inspiration while the others searched his face for some kind of a signal they weren't screwed. Suddenly, a bone-shattering, marrow-melting yell rent the big-sky-country air—a shrill cry so chilling rattlesnakes swallowed their tails and coyotes urinated in terror. Before the battle cry died away, wave after wave of shrieking savages leaped lemming-like from the top of the ridge and charged.

Divine inspiration hit Milton in a flash. "Run!" He slung the wounded superstar over his shoulder and headed toward the mountains.

With Milton in the lead, the twelve ran as a terrified pack. One hundred thousand settlement-seeking lawyers were quickly closing the fifty-yard gap between them.

"Run, Viv," Lance encouraged his friend. "Run, Phanny. Run Margaret. Run like the wind."

"I won't think of it now," Margaret thought as she fled. "I'll go crazy if I think about what they'll do if they catch me. I'll...why, I'll run home to Tara. I'll think about what to do tomorrow. After all, tomorrow is the first day of the rest of my life."

MOONLIGHT BOWL MANIFESTO

EPILOGUE

"Tut, tut, child," said the Duchess. "Everything's got a moral if only you can find it!"

>Lewis Carroll
>*Alice's Adventures in Wonderland*

BARBARA JONES

MOONLIGHT BOWL MANIFESTO

Barbara Jones

Barbara Jones was born in Chicago, but was living in California at the time. She spent the first eight years of her life in California and, many years later, returned to find her roots. What she found, instead, compelled her to write *Moonlight Bowl Manifesto* and move to Roswell, Georgia, where she now lives and writes.

Her father was a writer and Vice President and Creative Director for the J. Walter Thompson advertising agency. Her mother was a housewife and artist with a biting Irish wit that amused the neighbors and annoyed the hell out of her children. Barbara hopes she has inherited her mother's wit and her father's ability to temper that wit with gentle good humor. She is one of five siblings and numerous "strays" her mother adopted, including unwed mothers, runaways and throwaway children.

Barbara moved from California when she was eight and spent a few years in Wisconsin before relocating to Chicago where she was lucky enough to experience Mayor Daley's political machine, the 1968 Democratic National Convention, ethnic diversity and deep-dish pizza. She learned to drive at age twenty-seven after moving to the suburbs and unsuccessfully waiting two weeks for a bus.

She dabbled in the corporate world and developed her succinct writing style while editing three-page press releases to fit twenty-five-words-or-less formats. She honed her fiction skills by writing advertising copy and inspirational speeches for corporate executives. She weaned herself from the corporate teat by taking temp jobs and pursuing free-lance writing assignments. After failing the Kelly Services Computer Skills Test for Temporary Employees, she decided to devote herself to writing. Or, as her mother-in-law calls it "avoiding a real job."

Barbara now lives happily in a wooded suburb of Atlanta with her husband and fifty billion ants.

Coming soon from Russell Dean & Company, and Barbara Jones:

101 Gun and Pawn
By Barbara Jones

When Jack Lardner retires from a big city police department and moves to rural Arkansas, he expects to fish, hunt, and enjoy his family. He doesn't expect to open a pawn shop or find himself in the middle of a murder mystery. But that is exactly what happens in Barbara Jones latest work.

When Frank'n'Burt find a dismembered corpse stuffed in a cooler, the whole town buzzes rampant with speculation about not only who the murderer is, but who is murdered.

Jack's 101 Gun and Pawn Shop is a "rustic salon" for an eclectic cast of Barbara Jones' whacked-out characters. Meet Brody Tucker, a nineteen-year old mechanic with a thirty-two-year-old wife and an eight-year-old stepdaughter (do the math!); Frank and Burt, two old geezers who are together so much people refer to them collectively as Frank'n'Burt; Annabelle, a woman so insecure, she believes even Jesus only tolerates her; and Sweet Adeline and Harry Burke, a married pair of professional thieves who steal to order.

This is not a murder mystery, although there is a murder. This is not a story about a failed marriage, although that happens, too. It's not a story about a pawn shop, even if that's where most of the action takes place. This is an engaging story about people gettin' by and gettin' on, as only Barbara Jones can write it.
If you enjoyed Barbara's wry and witty assault on California political correctness in *Moonlight Bowl Manifesto,* you'll roar at her characters' antics as she takes a shot at life in a small southern town.